LOVE LETTERS BY THE SEA

SIREN'S RETREAT #4

ERICA RIDLEY

COPYRIGHT

ALSO BY ERICA RIDLEY

The *Dukes of War*:

The Viscount's Tempting Minx

The Earl's Defiant Wallflower

The Captain's Bluestocking Mistress

The Major's Faux Fiancée

The Brigadier's Runaway Bride

The Pirate's Tempting Stowaway

The Duke's Accidental Wife

A Match, Unmasked

The *Wild Wynchesters*:

The Governess Gambit

The Duke Heist

The Rake Mistake

The Perks of Loving a Wallflower

Nobody's Princess

***Rogues to Riches*:**

Lord of Chance

Lord of Pleasure

Lord of Night

Lord of Temptation

Lord of Secrets

Lord of Vice

Lord of the Masquerade

The *12 Dukes of Christmas*:

Once Upon a Duke

Kiss of a Duke

Wish Upon a Duke

Never Say Duke

Dukes, Actually

The Duke's Bride

The Duke's Embrace

The Duke's Desire

Dawn With a Duke

One Night With a Duke

Ten Days With a Duke

Forever Your Duke

Gothic Love Stories:

Too Wicked to Kiss

Too Sinful to Deny

Too Tempting to Resist

Too Wanton to Wed

Too Brazen to Bite

Magic & Mayhem:

Kissed by Magic

Must Love Magic

Smitten by Magic

LOVE LETTERS BY THE SEA

SIREN'S RETREAT #4

ACKNOWLEDGMENTS

Thank you to Grace Burrowes who jumped aboard the shared series idea without hesitation! Working with you has been a delight.

As always, I could not have written this book without the invaluable support of my editor and beta crew, with special thanks to Erica Monroe. You are the best!

I also want to thank my wonderful VIP readers, our Historical Romance Book Club on Facebook, and my fabulous early reader team. Your enthusiasm makes the romance happen.

Thank you so much!

CHAPTER 1

May 1818
Brighton, England

$\mathcal{M}$rs. Deborah Cartwright expanded her diaphragm, tipped her head back toward the chandelier, and let the notes fly.

It had been years since she was a celebrated soprano in the London opera, and the Sharp Tea Room in Brighton in no way resembled the footlights of a theatre stage, but as to the *feeling*... Oh, the feeling! Singing was joy and freedom. It was bits of her soul, escaping from her lungs note by note, to merge with the souls of everyone else present and fill *them* with joy as well.

The talented pianist to Deborah's side, Mrs. Allegra Sharp, was no mere accompanist. Deborah was accompanying *her*. Not that Allegra needed any help to enchant her audience. Locals and tourists alike crowded into the tea room at all hours of every day in the hope of catching the famed Allegra Sharp at her pianoforte.

When Allegra had heard Deborah sing, the pianist had begged to compose something original for Deborah that would showcase her soaring voice to its best advantage. They now had not one, but three songs in their repertoire, all of which engendered standing ovations from the delighted crowd...when Deborah could tear herself away from Siren's Retreat to come and sing, that was.

Being the sole proprietress of a large, busy inn with the best seaside views in all of Brighton was a lot of work—but it was also Deborah's true calling. As joyful and free as she felt when she gave herself over to song, it could not compare to the honor and wonder of her inn. It had been worth giving up a career in the opera fifteen years ago, and it had been worth it every minute since.

Siren's Retreat had given Deborah her one true love: ten glorious years with Mr. Harland Cartwright. Every season since they first opened their doors, the inn had brought love into the lives of its guests. Siren's Retreat—and Deborah herself— had become legendary for uniting hearts and making perfect matches.

That was what she *should* be thinking about: Bringing good fortune and true love to her paying guests. Not the handful of secret correspondence burning a hole in her reticule.

She'd recognized the handwriting on one of the missives at first glance. The mysterious, anonymous letter-writer with whom Deborah had been corresponding at first intermittently and now almost daily, for several months in a row.

In the empty space between letters, she couldn't possibly *miss* him. No matter what it felt like at times. They didn't even know each other's names! Their connection wasn't real at all. Just happenstance and a pile of post. Deborah *knew* that. And yet...

She let the final note hang in the air for a few extra seconds, then dashed to her abandoned chair in the corner of the tea shop like a child running toward a pile of sweets.

It was not candied peels Deborah hungered for, but rather the familiar script and easy charm of—

A loud, metallic clatter sounded from the kitchen. Followed by the unmistakable sound of breaking porcelain. The customers around Deborah exchanged fond glances. Frequent patrons of Sharp's Tea Room learnt to differentiate the unique signatures of every sort of accidental mishap.

"I hope it wasn't *my* tea," murmured a woman in a feathered bonnet.

"Oh, darling." Her companion's eyes crinkled. "That was *everybody's* tea."

Despite the doubtless truth to this statement, the customers' smiles only grew brighter. Sharp's Tea Room was renowned for its chef's unparalleled skill and his wife's incredible talent at the pianoforte, but some might argue the *real* reason tourists haunted the tables was in hopes of being present when Mr.

ERICA RIDLEY

Sharp and Mrs. Sharp locked eyes. That was the real magic.

John rushed out of the kitchen bearing a small tray in his hands, and wearing an apron covered in so many different substances that it was decorated with every color under the sun.

He set a steaming teapot down at Deborah's table and whispered, "There was a small issue with the *pâte à choux*. I may need five more minutes."

"It's no problem," she assured him. "Take your time."

Five minutes might give her a chance to read her letters before returning to the hustle and bustle of her inn.

"Thank you for understanding." John straightened and turned toward the pianoforte.

For a moment, Deborah—and likely everyone else watching as well—thought the silver tray would tumble from his fingers.

John had just glimpsed his wife again.

She was rising from the bench, which normally would cause the room to erupt in protest as guests pleaded with her to play just one more song.

But nothing could eclipse the way John and Allegra looked at each other. The tea room crackled with the strength of their connection. It was as if they were seeing each other for the first time. Love at first sight all over again. Two halves of the same soul.

Romantic sighs sounded throughout the large

salon, followed by several deeply impressed glances toward Deborah.

This was her doing. Or rather, the legend of Siren's Retreat in action.

A few short months ago, this perfect-for-each-other couple had been two complete strangers, who, like so many others before them, had booked a seaside holiday and found love instead. Deborah could fill a book with such success stories. Not that words on a page could ever compare to seeing true love unfold before one's own eyes.

Words on a page. Her gaze lowered to her reticule, and she drew out the small stack of correspondence with shaking fingers. Ridiculous to have shaking fingers! They weren't *love* letters. Her trembling was due to lack of tea cakes, not to the excitement of having a note from LostInLondon.

No one believed in the lifechanging magic of finding your One True Love more than Deborah.

This was because she'd already found hers. Married hers. Then buried hers. Harland's funeral was the worst day of Deborah's life, but the years before that had been nothing but pure bliss. She knew the power of love firsthand, which was why she and her inn sought to bring that magic to others.

As for Deborah herself, those days were over. She had *had* her one life-changing experience. That was it. Lightning did not strike twice. The phenomenon was called "One True Love" for a reason. It was not "The

First Of Multiple Potential Loves". The challenge was *because* there was only one perfect person out there for everyone. The magic came in finding them.

Now that her personal quest was over, she dedicated both Siren's Retreat and every spare second to helping others find the same wonderful, giddy madness.

None of which had anything to do with the letter in her hands. She didn't have *feelings* for Lost-InLondon. Not only was love relegated to Deborah's past. LostInLondon was just... words on a page. A stranger destined to remain a stranger. No one to start swooning over.

Their introduction hadn't begun with any particular fireworks, either. The local newspaper had a monthly column dedicated to extolling Brighton's healthful virtues...and an address at the local church to write to, if one had additional questions that weren't answered in the broadsheet.

Normally, the parson's wife handled the correspondence, but whilst she was lying-in for her third child, Deborah had briefly taken over the responsibility. It was simple. She needn't sign her responses, all of which were posted care of the newspaper. Most of the questions were easily answerable in a sentence or two, between attending to Deborah's normal duties at the inn.

And then. *And then.*

She broke the wax seal with a definitely-not-trembling finger and gently shook out the newest letter.

A flush crept up her neck at the sight of LostIn-London's familiar handwriting. This wasn't a *blush*. It was the warmth of friendship. No—not even friendship. The warmth of altruism, nothing more. And maybe a little intrigue. Perfectly aboveboard.

Ever since the address for inquiries first opened, the vast majority of letters came from those who clearly would never make the trip. LostInLondon was just another would-be guest who could not afford an actual holiday in beautiful, fashionable, expensive Brighton.

If Deborah's correspondence with him had gone beyond the usual—a short, efficient, facts-only paragraph in reply—and become, well, *this*... It was because LostInLondon was too kind and charming for her to respond with curt efficiency.

The truth was, Deborah didn't want to have done with their conversations. She wanted them to go on indefinitely.

She supposed, in a way, she had started it. Well, *he* had started it, by inquiring about Siren's Retreat, which was the most important part of Deborah's world. Of course her answering letter should include the most effusive picture possible. With each dip of her pen, she tried to paint in words how wonderful the Brighton air was, and how magical the views from every angle.

Over time, their letters changed until hers spoke as though LostInLondon accompanied her on her utterly normal days, which she tried to make sound as charming as possible—without giving away that she was Mrs. Deborah Cartwright, proprietress of Siren's Retreat, rather than Salt&Sea, temporary volunteer columnist for the local newspaper.

She wasn't misleading him...exactly. She was both things at once. But he might find her advice and assertions a *wee* bit biased if she admitted she also made her living from the tourists who chose her inn above all others.

So instead she talked about Brighton in general. The brisk, salty wind on one's face, the tangy taste of the air, the feel of the breeze rippling through one's hair before one makes a wild dash to recover one's bonnet before it floats away. The coffee rooms and tea rooms and assembly rooms. The seaside promenades and the evening waltzes. The delicious food and the friendly faces. What was there not to love about Brighton?

For his part, LostInLondon spoke of London in the briefest terms, if at all. A crowded, dirty city. Too much noise and chaos. Not enough hours in the day to do all the work assigned to him, and no chance at all to escape on a much needed holiday.

In every letter, LostInLondon thanked his darling Salt&Sea for making him feel as though he needn't travel from his desk to take in the sights at her side. He spoke so longingly, so poignantly, so romantically. Every paragraph sounded as though he knew her. As though he *missed* her. Which was not possible, since they had never met and would never meet. Yet Deborah knew just how LostIn-London felt, because she felt the same way herself.

Oh! She covered her mouth to hide a giggle at an amusing anecdote involving LostInLondon's high-spirited nephews' encounter with their neighbor's new litter of puppies.

She read the letter a second time, and then a third, imagining how he might react to each of her responses. But she would have to save letter-writing for later. It was time to return to her post at the inn. Deborah tried not to stay away from her station for more than an hour at a time. Guests might have need of her.

Before she left Sharp's Tea Room, however, she glanced at the other two letters in the pile.

Rubbish, both of them. More offers to purchase Siren's Retreat from her. Deborah crumpled them into a ball. As if she would ever sell!

This property had been in her husband's family for centuries. Generations of Cartwrights had lived here in this spot since long before Brighton became a health resort in the early 1700s. Her home was not just a living link she shared with her deceased husband. When they discovered they could not have children, the inn became their baby instead. They built it together, turning the property from a family estate to the bustling, renowned, rarely-with-a-vacancy Brighton destination it now was today.

There was also the small wrinkle that Deborah couldn't sell even if she wanted to. The property was entailed, meaning it went to the next male heir upon her husband's death. Luckily, Harland's brother Stanley was as proud of Siren's Retreat as

Deborah and Harland had been. Stanley was happy to lease the land to Deborah, out of respect for Harland as well as the important role Siren's Retreat played in the vibrant Brighton community they all loved so much.

Letter-writers like these rude investors intimated that a woman could not possibly have the knowledge or strength of character to run a business. Would it be better for all parties if a man who knew nothing about the guests, the location, or the legend took it out of her pretty little hands? Ha!

To his credit, Stanley hadn't once attempted to wrest control from Deborah, or to meddle in any manner. He knew as well as she did that no one could run Siren's Retreat with the same passion. It was built on love, and continued to bring that magic to all of its guests. The inn, like the memory of her late husband, was irreplaceable.

She would *never* let anyone take it from her.

CHAPTER 2

*O*n his return to the Earl of Edgewick's Mayfair residence, Mr. Patrick Gretham paused for a brief moment to watch the beleaguered nanny in the terrace home next door attempt to corral a rambunctious kitten and two equally rambunctious children in the front garden.

His lordship frowned on servants who paused in their labor, however briefly, and would have been quite put out indeed to see his trusted man of business—who should be setting an example for the rest of the staff—crouching in the grass to give the neighbors' new kitten a quick rub behind the ears.

Edgewick's wide-open study windows faced the large square below, affording him a clear and unobstructed view of his man of business tarrying unnecessarily. Or it would have done, if the earl were the sort to look out of windows. Luckily—or unluckily—for Patrick, when Edgewick was at home, he rarely glanced up from Patrick's financial reports long enough to do more than bark at the closest maid to refill his port.

From this, one might presume the earl to be a bit of a drunk and very much a misanthrope…and one would not be wrong in this assumption. But the Earl of Edgewick also bore a shrewd mind for business. He won far more than he lost at the gambling tables, and expected Patrick's performance with his lordship's investments to prove even more impressive.

After a final rub for the kitten, Patrick directed himself to the earl's front door. He straightened his spine and his cravat, removed his hat and his smile, then strode straight into Edgewick's study.

"You're late," the earl barked without looking up from his papers.

"I'm early," Patrick replied. It was why he had risked a moment of happiness with the kitten. "My errands took less time than expected."

"Because you did not have the right words to reach our aims?"

"Because strong-armed tactics were unnecessary." Patrick slipped a stack of signed contracts atop the pile Edgewick had been perusing. "I believe you'll find these in order and to your liking."

The earl harrumphed.

Patrick waited patiently, unruffled.

Patient and *unruffled* were the primary characteristics required of any soul hoping to remain a member of the Earl of Edgewick's staff. Along with *tenacious*, *ambitious*, and *unerring*.

Of the few remaining servants who were not dismissed in mortification within their first fortnight of service, most of the other workers rarely lasted more than a few months before stomping out the door in anger or fleeing the premises in tears.

Patrick possessed the dubious honor of having the longest length of employment for any of the earl's staff. If he made it all the way to five years—a few short weeks away—Patrick was due to receive his first raise in salary and a sizable bonus. So sizable, in fact, Patrick half-expected the earl to dismiss him from service, simply to avoid having to make good on the promise.

No other staff member had such a clause in their contract. No one else had dared to negotiate so brazenly on their own behalf.

The earl had been moments away from ejecting Patrick from the property for impertinence and presumption, when Patrick had pointed out that a man of business unafraid to make demands and take profitable risks was the *exact* sort of person Lord Edgewick ought to want out on the streets, negotiating on his lordship's behalf.

Arguably, the earl had agreed to the proviso largely because he hadn't expected Patrick to last *one* year, much less five. But here they were, each of them about to be significantly richer thanks to the other.

Edgewick glanced up from the papers. "The Marquess of Silverstone sold his shares?"

Patrick hid a satisfied smile. "Docile as a lamb, my lord."

The earl grunted.

Silverstone had been anything but docile, but Patrick had prevailed. He knew all the most vulnerable spots to poke. Before this post, Patrick had worked for Silverstone's father for fifteen years. Upon inheriting the marquessate, the heir had dismissed Patrick from service because he already had his own man of business, and did not see what advantage retaining his father's servant could bring.

Now he saw. And so did the Earl of Edgewick.

"Well done," his lordship said grudgingly, his compliments rare and far between. "Why are you still standing here? Have you no work to do at your desk? Shall I halve your hours and your wages?"

Patrick bowed. "You know where to find me, my lord."

His office was on the opposite side of the corridor, with much smaller dimensions and no view of the pretty green square at the front of the crescent.

Patrick did not mind such details. Upon stepping into the room, he spied the one thing he *did* care about, piled atop his desk: the latest post. He tossed his hat and gloves aside and flipped through the pile with keen anticipation until he came across the handwriting he'd most been hoping to see.

Salt&Sea had written another letter.

His entire body felt like a happy smile. Patrick should not be wasting his limited time with meaningless correspondence. He *knew* this. And yet...his exchanges with Salt&Sea had come to be one of the most meaningful parts of his life. He looked forward to her pretty, precise script the way flowers looked forward to rain in the spring. Each new drop gave him life.

His initial inquiry to the tourism column of the Brighton newspaper had been on behalf of the Earl of Edgewick. Research for another speculative investment venture. Edgewick's name was synonymous with audacity and ruthlessness, so Patrick had sent out tentacles anonymously so as not to tip his hand.

The person who answered his letter was so forthcoming and sweet, Patrick had written back a second time, then a third, a fourth. Somehow, he had lost track of how many letters had been exchanged (though they were all tucked in a locked box for safety.)

The careful interrogation had given way to casual conversation, then to long letters that began with "Darling Salt&Sea" and "Dearest Lost-InLondon".

He and Salt&Sea no longer waited to receive each other's response before sending a new letter, thus ensuring a happy morning delivery every day of the week.

Their correspondence was often Patrick's *only* interaction with someone who did not want something from him. Salt&Sea wasn't trying to negotiate an agreement or convince him of anything, other than the beauty and perfection of Brighton. Her letters brimmed with faithful, step-by-step recreations of outings along the promenade, cups of steaming tea sipped by sunrise, laughter spilling in through an open window.

The quotidian anecdotes were anything but mundane. Each one filled Patrick with such longing, it was as though his narrow office did not look out onto a brick wall, but upon the seaside resort of Brighton. He imagined the laughter spilling through open windows was hers, amused by some charming thing he had said. That the steaming tea was a service for two, as the morning light warmed their smiling faces.

Not that he had any idea what Salt&Sea's true name was, or what she looked like. Those details didn't matter. She could be ancient, or hideous, and he would feel the same way about her as he did now. Her letters proved she had a beautiful soul. That they connected at a level Patrick had not previously believed himself capable of and had no wish to lose.

As soon as his five-year bonus was deposited into his account, he intended to take a long overdue holiday to Brighton in the hopes of meeting Salt&Sea face-to-face. If the joyful spark between them was just as strong in person as it was in letters, Patrick had half a mind to—

"Mr. Gretham?" A terrified maid cowered in the open doorway. Miranda was not frightened *by* Patrick, but rather, *for* him. "His lordship is calling for you."

Bellowing, more like. Patrick could hear the muffled yells, now that his attention had been diverted from Salt&Sea's latest letter.

"I'll see him at once," he assured the maid.

But before he rose from his desk, Patrick retrieved his box of treasures. He lovingly tucked the newest letter into a well-read pile tied with twine, locked and replaced the box, then strode from the room to see what new calamity had his employer in a fresh tizzy.

"I've decided," the earl barked before Patrick had fully crossed the threshold.

Patrick held his tongue and waited. The reports on Edgewick's desk represented over a dozen projects and proposals in various stages, many of which were awaiting some sort of decision on behalf of his lordship. Whether this summons pertained to the shipping venture or the manu-factory—

"It has to be Brighton," Edgewick announced. "All of the other venues you scouted are grossly inferior."

Most of the other venues were locations the earl himself had insisted Patrick investigate, but this was not the moment to quibble. Edgewick had Patrick's full attention from the moment he'd uttered the word *Brighton*.

Obviously, it was the best place. For anything. For everything. Brighton was the only place with Salt&Sea.

"This provincial inn—" Edgewick stabbed his

finger at one of the documents. "—is the perfect spot for my new gaming hell."

"It has lovely views," Patrick said without thinking, recalling an off-the-cuff comment Salt&Sea had made in one of her letters. "Bright windows in every guest room."

"We'll knock them all down," the earl assured him. "We don't want gamblers wasting time relaxing in their guest chambers when they ought to be down in the gaming salons buying brandy and betting their inheritances."

Edgewick reaped hundreds of pounds a month from one of the most successful gaming hells in London. If one determined "success" by the percentage of patrons who stumbled out from its shadows penniless and ruined.

The earl leaned back in his chair, tapping the tips of his fingers together in satisfaction. "I'll no longer be limited to a minority stake in someone else's club."

This again. Edgewick despised being a small player in someone else's grand venture. Patrick often thought what the earl chased was not fortune but fame. He had no need of additional riches. He wanted to be renowned. And Patrick was to help him achieve it.

He nodded dutifully. "You'll own the entire establishment."

"*We* will own it, Gretham." The earl's eyes glittered.

Patrick shook his head to clear it. "What did you just say?"

"Your five years are coming up. I'm sure you thought I'd forgotten—"

Patrick doubted the Earl of Edgewick ever forgot a single detail from any contract he'd ever signed.

"—but I have been watching you with care, and am fully prepared to reward not just your acumen, but your continued loyalty, by showing you the same."

Edgewick, loyal to anything but the balance of his banking accounts?

Patrick stared at him in confusion. "My lord?"

"On the five-year anniversary of your employment as my man of business, you will receive the raise and the perquisites as specified in your original contract. I will repeat the gesture after ten years. As an added incentive, once you bring me the deed to this property—" The earl held the Brighton papers aloft. "—you will receive a two percent minority stake in the new venture, free and clear."

A minority stake. *Patrick.*

In what was certain to be the most successful seaside gaming hell in England's history.

"But, my lord," he stammered. "Why would you—"

"I am many things, but not a fool," the earl interrupted. "You have proven your worth to me. I shall not allow some other lord to poach you out from under me. By tying your fortune to mine, I ensure not only many more decades of your service, but also that you will put forth every effort required to turn this ridiculous 'Siren's Retreat' into a river of money for us both."

Patrick had no intention of being "poached" by a competing lord. A two percent stake was all but meaningless to the earl, but to Patrick it meant nothing short of complete freedom. Even if the new gaming club only performed half as well as expected, Patrick's percentage would generate more revenue in a single season than his entire annual salary working for the earl.

Meaning, he wouldn't *have* to keep working. Patrick could carry along fine with the gaming hell earnings alone…or eke out another five years, collect the *next* bonus, and retire in high style whilst he was still young enough to enjoy life.

A life he definitely would *not* be spending in a cramped little room in the back of the Earl of Edgewick's residence.

"Wait." Patrick's body filled with bubbles, like a bottle of champagne in danger of exploding. "Did you say…when I *bring* you the deed? From Brighton?"

"You'll go at once," the earl said briskly. "I don't care if the owner claims not to be selling the property. Everyone has a price. Find it, pay it, and bring me the signed contract. You have one month. Mind you don't shirk your other duties in the meantime. I shall expect to break ground on the new club before the end of the season."

An entire, glorious month. In *Brighton*.

The possibility of coming face-to-face with Salt&Sea filled Patrick with such unexpected joy, he nearly passed out from lack of oxygen.

Yes, yes, he knew there were no guarantees. He and his sweet-natured letter-writer could pass on the street and not know each other. Their epistolary relationship, their closeness, their *honesty*, was predicated on a foundation of anonymity. Patrick would not betray her trust by pressuring her into revealing herself before she was ready.

He wasn't ready, either. Once he had his five-year bonus in hand and his minority stake in the new club, he would no longer be fettered to the earl or to London. Patrick would be able to visit Brighton as long as he liked, and woo Salt&Sea as an independent gentleman. As *himself*.

Then again, in the meantime, if his darling Salt&Sea *were* open to the idea of sharing that tea-for-two in real life, rather than via the pages of a letter...

"Consider the contract signed, my lord." Patrick bowed. "I'll pack my valise posthaste and return with your deed in hand."

CHAPTER 3

"*D*on't forget the guest registry," Deborah murmured to her niece, Nancy, whose blue eyes immediately went wide with panic.

"The registry book! Yes! You must sign the log before you can have your key!" Nancy snatched the already-delivered key from a very startled guest.

Before Deborah could smooth things over, Nancy half-buried a plume in black ink and forced the sodden feather into the guest's hand.

Deborah retrieved the over-inked plume before it could splatter too much, and replaced it with a more appropriate writing implement. She gave the guests a friendly, confident, *everything-is-fine-here* smile.

She also gave him back his key.

"Nancy," she began gently, once the reception area was free of listening ears.

"I know." Nancy lowered her forehead onto the

counter in misery. "You were very clear on what to do, Aunt Cartwright. You've repeated the instructions a dozen times, and I understand perfectly in the moment. Then someone shows up with a reservation and I become so flustered…"

"Stand up straight, Nancy. You'll catch the rhythm." Eventually. Deborah hoped.

Nancy lifted her face from the reception counter. Her forehead was now dotted with stray splotches of ink from the over-dipped plume.

"I can do it," Nancy promised. "I'll be the best assistant you've ever had."

Deborah dipped a clean handkerchief in water and handed it to her niece. "Clean your face, darling."

Part of the problem was that Deborah had never *had* an assistant. Since its inception, she and her husband Harland had run Siren's Retreat together. After he died, Deborah had just…carried on. Alone. She had no one else to take up her time, so she spent every moment taking care of Siren's Retreat. It belonged to her and Harland. Letting anyone else in seemed like a betrayal.

But the legend of Siren's Retreat grew bigger with every passing year. So did the waiting list of guests hoping to reserve accommodations… As well as the endless tasks required to keep up with a constantly full inn of rotating guests, each with different needs at every hour of every day.

As much as it pained Deborah to admit, if Siren's Retreat were to remain the premier romantic hostelry destination in Brighton, she could not possibly do everything on her own.

Finding the right person to help, however, was even harder.

"I'm sorry," Nancy babbled as she smeared the ink stains about her face. Now she looked like a Dalmatian. "Let me try again. Here comes someone now. I won't disappoint you this time."

Deborah glanced through the mullioned window at the sunny street. The person approaching was not a guest, but the man who brought the morning post. She'd recognize his silhouette anywhere.

"Stay here," she told Nancy.

Deborah lifted the hinged section of the wide wooden counter and dashed past the small round tables decorated with today's newspapers to meet the postman at the door.

Might there be... Could there be... There was!

She pressed the letter from LostInLondon to her chest and twirled back to the counter—only to recall belatedly that today she had an audience.

Nancy's eyes were even wider than when she'd forgotten to have their guest sign the registry.

"What is it?" she whispered. "An unexpected inheritance?"

Considering Deborah had yet to *open* the letter, there was no practical way for her to intuit unexpected tidings.

Long before marrying Harland, Deborah had no remaining family members of her own, and therefore no one from whom to inherit anything at all, unexpectedly or otherwise. Even Harland had been unable to will her the inn directly. It was his brother, Nancy's father Stanley Cartwright, who controlled the lease and the land.

But none of that mattered. This was a letter from LostInLondon. It had arrived a full hour later than usual, causing Deborah to despair if she would receive word of him today at all. LostInLondon was such a part of her morning routine that it almost felt as if *he* were the assistant providing her company in the lonely gaps between customers.

"Just a letter," she said lightly. "From a friend."

He was *that*, at least. An epistolary friend, which if anything made their friendship deeper. As Salt&Sea, she could be more herself with LostIn-London than she could have ever been if they'd met somewhere ordinary, like at the assembly rooms or on the beach. He could not judge Deborah based on her name, her appearance, her address, her history, her manner. All he knew were her innermost thoughts. What could be truer than that?

She started to casually toss the unopened letter onto the countertop, then remembered the inkblots that had stained her niece's face. No doubt the ink had dried by now, but why take that chance? No sense waiting. Deborah leaned her shoulders against the wall and ripped open the wax seal.

Instantly, she was transported to London. The nephews and the puppies were at it again. Her fond smile widened with each new line. LostInLondon had such a charming way of relating even the smallest details. Or perhaps she was charmed by his insistence that the bucolic scenes he recounted could only be improved with her presence. That he wished she were watching the amusing spectacle by his side the same way Deborah secretly yearned for LostInLondon to be present in her life in more than mere words.

"It's a *love letter*," Nancy breathed.

Deborah jumped. She'd forgotten her niece's proximity again.

"It is no such thing," she said sternly, though her stomach had fluttered at the accusation.

Fluttered in *protest*. Not in agreement. How could it be a love letter if they never spoke of love? They'd never even met.

Yes, yes, she now addressed her letters to "my dearest" LostInLondon, making him only the second man to have earned the distinction of being Deborah's dearest anything. But that did not change the facts.

"Your Uncle Harland, God rest his soul, was and remains my one and only love," she assured her niece. "Most people aren't fortunate enough to experience what we had even once in their lives. I would never despoil the memory of what we had with some passing infatuation."

Right?

Nancy stared at her aunt with open skepticism, as though *Deborah*'s face were the one covered in tell-tale signs of inner turmoil. "If it's not a love letter, what is it?"

"Oh, nothing at all." Deborah gave the letter an airy wave. "Just the most ordinary, mundane conversation. Boring, really. He says… He…" She jerked the page up to her face with trembling fingers. "He's coming to Brighton!"

CHAPTER 4

*P*atrick watched from the carriage window with anticipation as Brighton came into view.

It was heady to think that he might brush shoulders with Salt&Sea, here in the seaside resort town she loved so much. They did not know each other's names or appearances, but a tiny, silly, romantic part of him could not help but hope that the strong connection they shared through their letters would flourish in the flesh. That they would somehow know each other at once, their souls as unmistakably identifiable as their handwriting.

Which brought him to another concern: their ongoing correspondence. Patrick did not want to miss a single word from Salt&Sea's pen.

To keep the sensitive inquiries he made for Edgewick anonymous, Patrick arranged any number of clandestine delivery methods, forwarding from one unrelated address to another before finding its way into his hands, so that the sender was unaware of the earl's connection.

In this case, Patrick's hands were here in Brighton. When Salt&Sea next wrote, he did not want to waste time chasing down a letter heading toward London when he was right here in the same town. Thus, before the driver even reached the hotel, Patrick stopped the carriage next to the post office and rushed inside to alter his standing instructions.

Rather than forward any post addressed to his pseudonym to an equally fictitious name with a London address, Patrick informed the administrator that he was in town on holiday, and would drop by in person every morning and afternoon to retrieve any correspondence. He added a generous vail to ensure confidentiality.

Retrieving letters in person was even *more* exciting than sitting at his desk hoping one of the earl's footmen would interrupt Patrick's work with the arrival of the post. This way, he would have the folded parchment in his hands within hours of it leaving Salt&Sea's fingers. Possibly even within minutes! Wouldn't that be marvelous?

He was so enamored by this idea, that as the carriage continued on toward the hotel, Patrick barely noticed the sea of faces outside the carriage window. Until he remembered that any one of them could be Salt&Sea. He abandoned all interest in Brighton landmarks at once, instead concentrating all of his focus on noticing and remembering as many passing countenances as possible.

The people that were clearly tourists would not be Salt&Sea. But any woman who looked like a local had some probability of actually being—

"We're here, sir." The driver stopped the carriage.

Here, unfortunately, did not mean Siren's Retreat. Patrick's interest in that inn had less to do with its impending purchase, and more to do with the obvious soft spot Salt&Sea held for the establishment. He should have liked to experience it through her eyes at least once before it became something completely different. But it was not to be.

Siren's Retreat was completely full, every room having been reserved months in advance. Patrick took the last rooms in an inn across the street. In a way, this was a much better vantage point. He was able to see the entirety of Siren's Retreat's main structure from the front windows of his guest chamber.

Besides, it wasn't as though Salt&Sea would be *inside* the inn. She lived in Brighton year-round, and must have a home or rent rooms in one of thousands of permanent residences scattered along the pretty streets.

Salt&Sea seemed to have a soft spot for almost every establishment in Brighton, Siren's Retreat being just one of many. There was a tea room she seemed to particularly favor, and a specific stretch of the beach with the best sunrise... Mayhap tomorrow morning, he could conveniently wander in that direction at the break of dawn?

Patrick brought into his guest chamber all the usual trappings he traditionally brought with him when traveling on mission for the earl, but could not help but feel something was missing.

Something romantic.

Not a *grand* gesture. Only a fool would bring diamonds for a woman whose name and face he did not know. But...a *small* gesture. Posies, perhaps. A new writing slope. Something small but meaningful, that he knew Salt&Sea would like.

Nonsensical, of course. He wasn't *courting* her. He might never ever be in the same room as her throughout the entire trip.

But the *next* trip... Ah, that's where Patrick's imagination really ran wild. As the earl's man of business—and bearing a stake in the new venture himself—Patrick would surely be sent to Brighton several times a year to oversee the transition from inn to gaming hell. Regular meetings with to the local manager to review his books.

Even if most of that could be accomplished remotely, Patrick would insist upon in-person visits. Once his stake in the new venture was firmly in hand, for example, if he were to meet a certain letter-writer face-to-face and discover that they did indeed suit very well... With the gaming hell operational, profits would roll in. Enough that Patrick wouldn't *have* to work for the earl or live in London if he didn't want to.

He could offer Salt&Sea a wonderful life right here.

Patrick freshened from the carriage ride, then set out from his hotel, guidebook in hand.

He did not need the guidebook. He'd already read, assimilated, memorized, and compiled reports on every word that had ever been written about the seaside town. But he was not to announce himself as Mr. Gretham, the Earl of Edgewick's man of business, quite yet.

First, he needed to confirm all the relevant facts about Siren's Retreat that were *not* printed in any newspaper or guidebook, in order to strengthen his negotiating position when presenting the earl's offer to the current owner.

A Mr. Stanley Cartwright had inherited the inn from an elder brother. He did not appear to be particularly sentimental about the property, which worked to Patrick's advantage. The man seemed to know little-to-nothing about how it was run, and cared only about the modest rents its lease brought in. Compared to those sums, the earl's proposal would seem fortuitous, indeed.

On his way across the street, Patrick smiled at every woman he passed, in case it was Salt&Sea. Silly, of course. If he didn't know which lady was Salt&Sea, Salt&Sea certainly would not know that the stranger smiling at her was LostInLondon. But wouldn't it be an amusing tale, when at last they *did* meet?

I remember you! she would say with a delighted little laugh. *I was having my afternoon stroll, when suddenly there was this smile, from a stranger who I felt I knew as well as my own self—*

Or perhaps that was what Patrick was hoping would happen to *him*. That one of these strangers would smile back, and he would feel instant recognition all the way to his soul. That there *was* something more to look forward to in life than stock in a gaming hell and a raise in salary: Someone to share it with.

Someone he loved.

After two decades of spending every moment fulfilling the whims of powerful lords, Patrick wanted the power to indulge his own desires. Not in a transactional manner, with a courtesan or mistress. But in an "I *choose* to spend time with you" way.

To see the same face morning after morning because that face brought happiness. To share a cup of tea in the quiet of dawn because quiet and a cup of tea were *enough* when shared with the right person. To not need anything else, because the person next to you filled your empty spots the same way you filled theirs.

Perhaps he was a fool to believe in love like that. In forty years, he'd certainly seen no sign of it. But what was the point of driving himself so hard for two decades, if not to have someone with whom to share the fruits of his labor?

"Soon," he muttered under his breath as he pushed open the door to Siren's Retreat.

Once the gaming hell was in place and his five-year bonus safely in his banking account, Patrick could take a proper holiday with the person who would give his life a richness no raise in salary on earth could provide.

A brief tussle broke out behind the reception counter. The older of two attractive ladies elbowed the younger in the ribs whilst clearing her throat meaningfully and tilting her head in his direction.

A very pretty head, Patrick could not help but notice. Dark brown hair was pulled into what had presumably started the day as a no-nonsense, matronly bun, but was now softened by carefree curls escaping wherever they could. Her mouth was firm, but smiling. Her eyes, a bright blue even more brilliant than the sea or the clear skies overhead. Eyes that radiated sunny days, even while indoors. He could not look away. She was the most beautiful woman he could ever remember seeing.

The younger lady relinquished the broom she'd been using to sweep the floor and took a deep breath before turning to Patrick. "Welcome to Siren's Retreat, sir. How do you do? May I help you?"

He forced his attention to the girl who had spoken. She was young enough to be his daughter. Possibly *was* the daughter of the lady with the captivating eyes. Who was therefore probably married. And even if she wasn't, was most definitely not the reason Patrick was surveilling the inn. He was to gather intelligence to aid the Earl of Edgewick's impending negotiations and purchase of the property.

Patrick held up his guidebook. "I hear Siren's Retreat has the best views in Brighton."

"Um," said the younger one, and glanced over her shoulder for assistance.

The older woman tried to convey an entire monologue in the set of her pink lips and the flashing of her light blue eyes, to no avail. The hapless assistant looked tongue-tied and terrified. As though the girl had never once looked outside of a window, and hadn't the least notion what she or Patrick might see if they did.

After an interminable standoff, the woman with the soft brown hair spun away from her charge and fixed Patrick with a sunny smile of infectious good cheer. He could not fathom why anyone should wish to waste time looking outside the inn's many windows, when one could gaze at a face as pleasant as this one instead. Her sparkling gaze felt like the warm sun on a cool day. Her smile, able to brighten any darkness.

"I am Mrs. Cartwright." Her musical voice was a low alto that caressed his skin like soft satin.

"I am the proprietress of Siren's Retreat. My niece, Miss Nancy Cartwright, is assisting me in between bouts of shyness."

"I'm not shy," said the niece. "I just don't want to say the wrong thing."

"As long as your answers are true, they can't be wrong. *Are* there good views from here?"

"The best," said the niece. "But one could argue that the legend indicates guests should not be gazing through the glass. The love they're looking for will be found right under this roof, not on the streets outside."

"I'm not a guest," Patrick said helpfully. "I'm new to Brighton." He paused. *Mrs.* Cartwright. Married. Unless… "Is *everyone* under your roof looking for love?"

"Yes," replied the niece, at the same time Mrs. Cartwright said, "No."

Ah. She had understood he had wondered about her, specifically, and was letting him know she was unavailable. Not that her status came as a surprise. One look at those bewitching eyes was enough to make any man's heart flutter, but the sound of her silken voice could enchant him completely. She would have had no trouble attracting suitors.

"Those who have already found love need search no longer," Mrs. Cartwright clarified apologetically. "I, like many of my guests, have been blessed in this manner."

Happily married, then. Patrick smiled at her good fortune. "The legend in action?"

"The very first perfect pair," she agreed, smiling back.

Such a lovely smile. It must scramble the brains

of anyone on the receiving end, man or woman, adult or child. Patrick tried to concentrate on his task, wracking his mind for details about the family. Mrs. Cartwright hadn't given her first name. He assumed she and the niece were the same Cartwrights as the Stanley Cartwright who owned the property.

Here, he would need to tread carefully. There was a treasure trove of knowledge on the other side of the counter. No one would have better ammunition—er, *insight*—about the landlord of the property than the family members who were tenants.

"Woefully," he said, "my guidebook only contains a few paragraphs about Siren's Retreat. Might one of you ladies be willing to give me a brief tour to show me what I've been missing?"

CHAPTER 5

*D*eborah couldn't stop staring at the strikingly handsome gentleman with the well-read guidebook. There was something about him that seemed familiar. Yet she was certain she'd never seen him before in her life.

He looked nothing like her husband. Like Deborah, Harland hadn't even been twenty at the time of their union, and had remained baby-faced for most of their too-short marriage. Harland's first gray hair had appeared mere weeks before he consumed the walnut that stole his life.

This man's chestnut hair was shot through with silver. His warm eyes were a hazel-ish brown, and decorated at the corners with many fine lines, indicating the smile on his face was not reserved for Deborah alone. He was well tailored in expensive clothing, more in line with the apparel worn by the inn's aristocratic customers than the capabilities of Deborah's pocketbook.

Oh, she supposed she could afford a fancy gown or two. Incongruously, she wished she were wearing something a bit more stunning than a serviceable morning gown of plain brown muslin. But why dress up when she was rarely gone from the inn longer than it took for tea at Sharp's or a quick peek at the sunset on the beach?

"I'm sorry," said Nancy. "There's no sense in wasting time with a tour when we're already booked up for the rest of the season—"

Good God, had Deborah actually said *no* answer was wrong, as long as it was true?

"I'd be honored to give a complete tour," she interrupted, sending Nancy a pointed glance that was supposed to mean, *We have openings* next *year* and *This well-heeled gentleman can clearly afford to book in advance—or works for someone who does.*

Nancy stared back at her as if Deborah's countenance indicated nothing more than a light case of indigestion.

"That's wonderful," said the man. "Thank you."

"Are you planning future travel here, Mr…"

"Gretham." His gaze did not waver. "I hope to return, yes. But it is my employer who has entrusted me to scout the perfect property."

Ha! A wealthy employer, exactly as Deborah had guessed. Given the inn's reputation, likely a lord with daughters to marry off. The best kind of client: money no object, and free to stay all season. She sent a *Now do you see?* glance toward Nancy, who

43

clearly did not understand the nuance of the situation at all.

Rather than attempt to relax Mr. Gretham with assurances he had indeed found the most well-appointed rooms in all of Brighton, Nancy looked ready to brain him with the broom handle for daring to suggest there had ever been room to doubt, and that he required a tour to prove it.

"Of course Siren's Retreat is the best," Nancy sputtered. "The guidebook in your hand says so. Can't you read? People come from every corner of England to find love and inspiration here, and if you cannot recognize the absolute perfection right in front of your eyes—"

"That's enough, Nancy," Deborah hissed in alarm. She lifted the counter and hurried over to Mr. Gretham before he could run off and tell his employer Siren's Retreat was run by unhinged creatures wielding broomsticks. "Please mind the reception area whilst I show Mr. Gretham about the property."

With luck, no one would require assistance in Deborah's absence. All the summer guests were already checked in for the season. The hour was late enough in the afternoon that even those who had returned at dawn from dancing all night in the assembly rooms had already awoken and gone out again in search of a new day's entertainments. With the inn so calm and quiet, it was actually the perfect moment to give a prospective guest a grand tour—presuming her niece had not turned him away.

"If we begin in this direction," she began as though her niece's loyal outburst had never occurred, "you can see how these south-facing windows not only let in plenty of light, but also afford an absolutely breathtaking view. There's the beach and promenade below, the vast sea along the horizon, and in just a few hours when the sun begins to set, the colors reflect in the clouds..."

Mr. Gretham nodded at all the right points, and dutifully glanced out each window when encouraged to do so, but otherwise did not seem to share the same concerns as most prospective guests. There were no questions about her staff, or the softness of the mattresses. Deborah might have feared she was boring the poor man right out of a sure reservation, except that his magnetic attention rarely left her face.

"Do you often go on such expeditions for your employer?" she asked.

"Always." The edges of his eyes crinkled. "I sometimes think he would not leave the comfort of the armchair in his study if I were not there to assure him the corridor to the dining room was perfectly passable, and that breaking his fast with a good meal would put him in a humor to better win at cards."

"Card-playing in the early morning?" she said with faux shock. "How scandalous!"

"Oh, *never*," he assured her. "'Morning' is when my employer goes to bed. He is too much a gentleman to rise for breakfast before noon, and even that hour is reserved for special occasions."

"Does that mean *you* rarely rise before noon?" she teased.

"Madam, it means I never *sleep*." His hazel eyes took on a roguish glint. He lowered his voice conspiratorially. "And that I am no gentleman."

She blushed despite herself, which was ridiculous. He was being silly, not flirtatious. She had started it, with her questions. Usually, she did not ask guests—or potential customers—anything of a personal nature. Only in her daily correspondence with LostInLondon could she be curious without fear of recrimination.

It made no sense that she would feel free to take the same friendly liberties with Mr. Gretham as though they'd known each other for months, and not mere minutes.

Deborah collected herself and concentrated on securing the reservation.

She had given such tours so many times that she didn't need to think about the words. Her legs knew where to walk, her hands knew where to gesture. Siren's Retreat *was* magnificent. With or without its legendary ability to matchmake those who stepped inside, its luxurious rooms and unparalleled vistas made it one of the best places from which to enjoy Brighton.

The question was whether Mr. Gretham saw it as she did.

He touched one of the walls and glanced toward

the ceiling as if judging the sturdiness of the building itself.

"You'll find the construction more than solid," she assured him. "This property has been in my husband's family for generations. We take great pride in its maintenance and upkeep."

He tapped the wall with his knuckles, and then nodded. "What is the maximum capacity of the mews behind the building?"

Good heavens, how rich *was* his employer? Was the extended family planning to bring every horse and carriage in their collection?

She calculated quickly in her head. "Well, each of the stalls is designed for…"

The questions came fast and thick now—if completely unlike any doubts she'd ever had to assuage for any of her prior customers.

Mr. Gretham seemed uninterested by the depth and expertise of her kitchen, or the extra touches for flair and comfort found in each guest chamber. His questions centered more on the logistics of the location itself, how simple it was to arrive on foot or by carriage, the dimensions of the various salons, the maximum capacity for simultaneous visitors.

Perhaps his employer wasn't merely hoping to marry off a daughter or two, but host an entire wedding party here in Brighton. It would be a miracle to book the whole property for a full season all at once!

"There are a finite number of guest rooms," she was forced to admit, "but we have several additional private cottages, and plenty of pretty garden with space for a large tent for entertaining. If your employer wishes to rent tables and chairs..."

Mr. Gretham listened with rapt attention, as though memorizing every word she said.

Deborah was not unused to spellbound reactions in crowds when performing a solo on stage, but not when discussing the finer points of mullioned windows and decorative molding.

Though her answers were well-practiced and automatic, there was nothing routine about the way Mr. Gretham's warm brown eyes fixed her with his full concentration. Or the strange flutter in her belly in response to being the object of such all-consuming focus.

Soon, they were no longer striding through the corridors, but sitting side-by-side on the edge of the uppermost bay window, overlooking the sea. Arguably the prettiest view in the inn...and neither of them were looking out the window. They faced each other instead, sunlight the only substance between them, their knees almost-but-not-quite touching.

When had they ceased talking about the inn and begun sharing about themselves?

"No pets?" he asked.

"No time," she admitted.

He pressed a hand to his lapel in shock. "No time to rub the ears of a puppy?"

"No time to clean up its mess," she clarified with a laugh. "You met my new assistant. Perhaps once

Nancy feels comfortable behind the counter, I will be able to carve out a few idle moments here and there into my day. I would like that."

"It may happen sooner than you think. Then what will you name your puppy?"

"Who said it will be a puppy? Perhaps I want a kitten. Or an owl."

He nodded. "What will you name your owl?"

"Rosencrantz," she answered with a straight face. "Or Mildred."

"Have two owls," he suggested. "Why limit the possibilities?"

"I do have two arms," she mused. "One could perch on each wrist."

"Like a fur muff! Except feathers. And alive. You could train them to attack your enemies."

"I haven't any enemies," she said with a laugh.

"You could make some, just for owl-attacking purposes. Nothing deadly! Just a swirl of feathers and a bit of aggressive screeching. No one would dare naysay you ever again."

"But then I would be known as the Owl Lady, and not the True Love Lady," she pointed out. "Who would journey to Brighton to see me then?"

"If you think a woman wearing two attack owls as fashion accessories is *less* interesting, then you vastly underestimate the English public. You'll have to employ *extra* attack called Guildenstern and Alfred just to give Rosencrantz and Mildred a few hours' rest."

Before she knew it, a quarter hour turned into half an hour, and then a full hour.

"You've lived here all your life?" he asked.

"Most of my adult life. Now that it's home, I never wish to leave."

"Brighton is as wonderful as they say?"

"It truly is. It feels like a small village when the tourist season is over, and a big city when everything is in full swing. I know every inch of this town."

His eyes twinkled at her. "*Every* inch?"

She grinned at him. "Test me."

"The best place for tea?"

"Sharp's Tea Room."

"Coffee?"

"Old Ship Inn."

"Fish?"

"Straight from the boats first thing in the morning. Don't dally past dawn."

"Best time for a dip?"

"Between seven and nine in the morning, but that is the wrong question. If you can swim, avoid the bathing machines altogether and enjoy the western section of beach directly."

"What's wrong with the eastern side?"

"That section is for women. The division gives each sex their privacy."

"What about the best gaming tables? Where do those with deep pockets find a rubber of whist?"

"Card rooms are available at either assembly rooms. There is also often play found at…"

As she explained the favorite gentlemen's haunts of Brighton, Deborah could not help a small frisson of disappointment. Nancy might be right that LostInLondon could walk through the door at any moment, but this man certainly wasn't him. After the many letters exchanged, LostInLondon could likely rattle off the top seaside sights just as easily as Deborah could.

Unless he *hadn't* read and reread those letters with care, as he'd claimed. Perhaps he kept up correspondence with dozens of lonely widows all over England, and Deborah—

Deborah was not lonely. Her life was dashed full, thank you very much. Brimming with activity. Overflowing, even. If LostInLondon's apparent affection for her was less than sincere, well, she didn't need him anyway. Wasn't even *looking* for someone.

She would do well to center her attention on Mr. Gretham, the dapper flesh-and-blood gentleman before her—and the future windfall if a wealthy family reserved all of her best rooms for the entire next season.

"Do you know the number of guests your employer intends to bring on his next visit?" she asked, as casually as she could. Sometimes, the implication that there would be no free rooms remaining if one did not act quickly was enough to win the reservation. "Or the dates of his stay?"

"I do not." Mr. Gretham's intense, hazel-brown

eyes held hers. "But I am looking forward to my own return to Brighton."

"Oh! I did not mean…"

But of course, she *had* meant that his employer's large family and equally large pockets were more of interest than the man before her. Her cheeks heated with embarrassment. She never spoke so carelessly to her guests. Even more proof that LostInLondon was a distraction she could ill afford.

Mr. Gretham's smile was easy and unconcerned. "If you did not peg me as a person likely to take an extended holiday, you are far from mistaken. I cannot recall the last time I had two free days in a row, and I have never taken a true holiday in my life. I am planning to change that next year."

She touched her throat. Many people could not afford expensive holidays, but to never even have two days in a row to call one's own… "Surely you needn't wait until *next* year to enjoy some much-deserved rest. May has barely begun. Is there no hope of a few days' relaxation?"

He tilted his head. "When is that last time *you* took a holiday from your hotel?"

"A holiday *away* from my inn?" She stared at him in incomprehension. Ever since Siren's Retreat had become Deborah's sole responsibility, she scarcely left its well-groomed grounds for more than an hour or two at a time.

His eyes held sympathy, not mockery. "Perhaps you are the one most in need of a holiday."

She shook her head. He did not understand.

This inn was her last tie to the past, and her only legacy for the future. She had no husband, no children. Siren's Retreat was everything. She could never walk away from it without feeling like she was leaving part of herself behind. Deborah *was* every window and every rafter and every stone holding up the inn all around them. Just like Siren's Retreat was the foundation that held *her* steady and gave her life meaning.

The church bells outside rang the hour, interrupting their banter, and forcing them both to realize how much time they'd spent doing nothing.

For Deborah, it had been one of the best afternoons in recent memory.

By the somewhat mystified look in Mr. Gretham's eyes, he was just as startled to be more taken by her than by Siren's Retreat.

"Thank you for the tour of your lovely property, Mrs. Cartwright. I don't suppose you offer tours of the town as well?"

CHAPTER 6

as the handsome gentleman flirting with Deborah, as it sometimes seemed? Or was he just amiable? It had been so long since she had last participated in a flirtation that she feared she had lost the knack to tell the difference.

Mayhap that was her problem with LostInLondon. He was being friendly, not flirtatious, and *she* was the one who was letting herself be distracted by a man she didn't even know all over again.

This behavior would not do. She would be firm with LostInLondon in her next letter. If he asked to meet, she would categorically decline. Siren's Retreat needed its proprietress to give it and its customers her undivided attention, not moon about like an adolescent miss with a glass of ratafia and a book of bad poetry.

"I am sorry," she told Mr. Gretham. "I do not give tours of Brighton. If you want to explore the town, you can either find someone else or follow your guidebook. But if you have any further questions about Siren's Retreat, you need only say the word, and I will be more than happy to attend to any concerns."

A heartbeat passed before he shook his head and gave a charmingly self-effacing smile. "Of course. It was silly to think...but I won't keep you any longer."

The truth was, she had never let Nancy alone behind the counter for so long, and wasn't certain it would still be standing. Quickly, she led him back toward the reception area. "Would you like me to place you or your employer's name on the list of potential guests for next year?"

An impossible-to-interpret shadow crossed Mr. Gretham's handsome face. Not quite a frown, but... yes, definitely a frown. Without fail, everyone who had ever taken a turn about Siren's Retreat had been eager to make a reservation. Mr. Gretham, however, was somehow insufficiently moved. She could feel the rejection coming even before his firm lips formed the first syllable.

"No," he said softly. "That won't be necessary. Thank you for your time, Mrs. Cartwright."

"Come back soon," she said, though they both knew he wouldn't. He was a nice man and this was a nice property. They just weren't meant for each other.

Mr. Gretham bowed and swept out through the door—only to hold it open for a pretty, round-cheeked figure making her way in. Deborah's other niece, Sybil, who was three years younger than Nancy.

"Have you come to collect your sister?" Deborah glanced at the tall-case clock. "It's a little early, isn't it?"

"It's Father," Sybil answered. "He wishes to speak to you."

Deborah bit back a sigh. "Now?"

Sybil nodded. "Now."

Stanley Cartwright, the girls' father and Deborah's brother-in-law, was a decent sort. He was not particularly sentimental in most things, but he renewed Deborah's lease every five years out of respect for the relationship she had shared with Stanley's brother Harland. For that alone, she would drop whatever she was doing when summoned and make the trip across town at once.

"Can you keep your sister company until I return?"

Sybil's face lit up. She was eager to leave the schoolroom and try her hand at being Deborah's assistant, too. Sybil had been disappointed to be told she was still too young to mind the reception area by herself. Surely if the two girls were there *together*, nothing much could go awry.

Right?

As she tied on her bonnet, Deborah went over the rules one more time. Once one or more of her nieces was properly trained and competent, perhaps Deborah *would* take a few hours off here and there without worrying that her beloved inn would crumble without her here, holding it up.

How long would it take before Nancy and Deborah both felt comfortable leaving Nancy behind the counter alone? A few more weeks? Months? Years?

Did Deborah even *want* to leave the inn in someone else's hands, no matter how capable they were, even for a moment?

AT HER BROTHER-IN-LAW'S RESIDENCE, Deborah was shown straight into his study, where Stanley was seated behind a large mahogany desk.

"Here's the situation," he said, skipping all pleasantries. Stanley was very efficient like that. Deborah appreciated the trait. His disinclination to waste time would let her hurry back to her inn all the faster. "Your current lease ends at the end of May."

She nodded. "Yes. I would like to renew for another five years. Or for a full decade, if you're amenable. I'm happy to sign straight away."

He steepled his fingers. "The rent will more than double in price."

"More than...what?" Deborah's voice went blank. The words made no sense. Stanley had given his brother a fair price, and had honored those terms for his brother's wife ever since. They were *family*.

"I realize you won't be able to afford it," Stanley

continued without changing expression. "I allowed you to pay less than market value for as long as I could. As a recent widow, you had few options, and I felt I owed as much to my brother. But five years have passed. Ten years of missed financial opportunities. The land you are using—"

"It's not...it's not *land*," Deborah stuttered. "It's Siren's Retreat. It's part of Brighton. It's part of Harland and part of me. It's—"

"It is part of my limited assets, and currently a poor investment," Stanley interrupted. "I have a family to consider."

"Am I...not...family?" she whispered.

"I have a wife and three young daughters to provide for. If I sell that property rather than rent it—"

"*Sell* Siren's Retreat?" she gasped. No. *Never*.

Good God, he was serious. Deborah couldn't afford to buy the inn from him, which would mean losing control of her home to some stranger, who would never run the property as well as she could. The quality of the retreat...the cherished clients... all the memories...

"I know you have a family of your own," she said quickly. "I'm trying to provide for them, too. Nancy is currently training to be my assistant—"

"Nancy shouldn't have a post at all," Stanley said firmly. "She wouldn't need to turn elsewhere for pin money if the hotel's landlord—*me*, her father— ceased playing charity, and charged what the property was worth."

Deborah said nothing. How could she argue? Every word was true.

"Listen." Stanley gentled his voice and lowered his steepled fingers. "It's not personal—"

"It is personal," she muttered. "Siren's Retreat *is* me. It's also all we have left of your brother."

A low blow. Not that she need have wasted her efforts on blatant emotional manipulation. Stanley's mind was already made up.

"I'm sorry," he said in the tone people took when the only thing they were sorry about was that you were continuing to waste their time. "As my brother's widow, I *am* giving you the courtesy of first rights to renew your contract. But if you are unwilling or unable to meet the new terms, I have other, more lucrative offers here on my desk. As head of household, as a husband and as a father of three girls, it would be an unthinkable breach of duty for me not to consider—"

"I'll pay it," she said quickly. If she raised prices, effective immediately... And landed a string of wealthy clients... "I won't just meet your terms. I'll prove to you Siren's Retreat is the *only* offer worth considering."

His expression wasn't just disbelieving. Stanley looked sorry for her. As if he'd already determined she would fail, and was just waiting for her to realize it too and give up.

"The only offer worth considering?" he repeated with a chuckle. "If you can convince me of that, I'll even relax the terms of the new lease."

"You'll see," she assured him, despite the panic crawling from every pore. Siren's Retreat was half-booked already for next year—at *last* year's rates. She would have to fill the rest of the room at astronomical prices indeed to make up the difference. "I'll have your proof and the next quarter's rent by the end of the month."

Starting with the only lead she had: Mr. Gretham and his wealthy employer.

CHAPTER 7

*P*atrick strolled about the exterior of Siren's Retreat early the next morning, pencil in hand, making notes on what renovations would need to take place to turn the placid, cozy inn into a bustling gaming hell.

He was to take his plans to a meeting with the current landowner, a Mr. Stanley Cartwright, later today. They were at the stage of negotiations wherein the selling party pretended not to be in the market to sell.

Theater, of course. The very fact that Cartwright had agreed to hold the meeting meant he was tempted by the offer. And where there was temptation, there was a price. All Patrick had to do was find the lowest possible number that would cover Cartwright's emotional quibbles about selling a property he'd inherited and never lifted a finger to manage, and *voilà*—the deed would belong to the Earl of Edgewick.

Patrick had completed so many transactions like this one over the past five years, he could negotiate in his sleep. Made all the easier by the earl's deep pockets, of course. If he wished, Patrick could walk into the meeting and let Cartwright name his own price. The man's wildest sally was unlikely to come anywhere close to what Edgewick was willing to spend to get what he wanted.

Hell, Patrick could probably purchase the Royal Pavilion from the Prince Regent himself if Edgewick took a strong enough fancy to it. Compared to that, maneuvering Stanley Cartwright would be simple. The man *wanted* to be convinced. And nothing convinced sellers better than piles of dazzling gold.

"Are you an artist?" quavered a voice.

Patrick glanced up to find a pair of elderly women watching him with curiosity. "Am I a what?"

"An artist." The older lady with a lace parasol gestured at the notebook in his hand. "Are you sketching? It is a lovely property."

Patrick couldn't well admit he was deciding which walls to knock down first, so he closed the book and bowed instead. "I have never seen a finer view."

The lady with a bird on her bonnet cackled. "That is the romantic irony of Siren's Retreat."

"Romantic irony?"

"Every window on the property had a beautiful view of Brighton," Lace Parasol explained. "But as any local knows—"

"And tourists," added Bird Bonnet. "They journey from miles away to be part of the story."

"—it is what you find *inside* that is the real treasure."

"True love," Bird Bonnet explained, in case Patrick had somehow not heard the legend printed in every guidebook about Brighton.

The Earl of Edgewick could not wait for the new gaming hell to take top billing instead. No, not the gaming hell—Edgewick wanted *his* name listed in every guidebook as an arbiter of taste and fashionable entertainment. The earl didn't give a fig about any legend but his own.

"True love," Patrick repeated noncommittally. "Is that right."

"It's a fact," said Lace Parasol. "The first love story was Harland and Deborah Cartwright themselves."

"Love at first sight, and *still* in love." Bird Bonnet gave a romantic sigh.

Patrick frowned. "I thought the husband died."

"Five years ago this spring," Lace Parasol agreed.

"Which changes nothing," Bird Bonnet added. "True love never wanes nor perishes. Their bond is immortal. Once a match is made at Siren's Retreat, the souls are forged together as one for all eternity. Cupid himself—"

Either these ladies had memorized the overwrought prose gushing about the inn in local guidebooks…or they had been the ones to *write* it. Patrick bit back his amusement.

"You'll never find a more loyal wife than Deborah Cartwright," Lace Parasol said. "No one can replace her dear husband—"

"No *human*," Bird Bonnet clarified. "She's every bit as devoted to her inn."

"I thought it wasn't her inn," said Patrick. "Doesn't Stanley Cartwright own and lease the land?"

"That doesn't make it not *hers*," Lace Parasol snapped.

"Well," murmured Patrick. "Except for technically. And legally. And every other recognized definition of ownership."

"Oh, for heaven's sake." Bird Bonnet scoffed. "Have you been talking to *Stanley*? That man has never understood why sentimental value is every bit as important as financial value."

Perhaps because one could not retire or go on holiday or even purchase a new pair of boots with an empty pocketbook full of *sentimental* value.

"Besides," said Lace Parasol. Her voice hushed as if imparting a momentous secret. "Deborah Cartwright is the titular siren."

Bird Bonnet nodded. "Right there in the name. What further proof could anyone need as to whom the property belongs?"

"If the Prince Regent christens his next boat 'the Beau Brummell', that doesn't mean the boat belongs to Brummell," Patrick pointed out. "And aren't sirens mythological creatures that lure unsuspecting men to certain doom?"

"Lovely, enchanting creatures," Bird Bonnet snapped.

"Famed for the unhappiest of endings." Patrick made an apologetic face. "I'm afraid the legend is fiction, ladies. All legends. By definition."

Lace Parasol glared at him. "This one is not! Granted, Deborah had no idea that walnut would lead Harland to his doom—"

"Not her doing," Bird Bonnet agreed. "Everyone at the assembly room that night was served the same dish. No one else reacted in such a violent manner."

"—but theirs was and is true love," Lace Parasol finished firmly. "She is as in love with her husband today as she was the day they first met. The same can be said for the dozens of matches made at Siren's Retreat."

"Hundreds of matches," Bird Bonnet said.

"Thousands," said Lace Parasol. "Siren's Retreat is as irreplaceable as our resident siren herself. So don't think you can muscle in here and worm your way into Deborah's heart, when it fully belongs to Harland—"

"What?" Patrick sputtered. "I'm not *flirting* with her. You'll note I'm not even *inside* the inn. Mrs. Cartwright has no idea I—"

"We saw you yesterday," Lace Parasol informed him.

Bird Bonnet nodded. "In the late afternoon, you can see right through the stairwell windows."

"Cozy," said Lace Parasol. "Too cozy."

"Talking her up," said Bird Bonnet.

"Standing too close," said Lace Parasol.

"Staring too intently," Bird Bonnet agreed. "Inappropriate cow eyes."

"I believe the term is *calf's eyes*," Lace Parasol whispered. "Cows are female."

"Those are the eyes he was making at her," Bird Bonnet whispered back. "You could practically hear him moo in appreciation." She sniffed. "Not even a paying guest and trying to make himself part of the legend."

"Well, you won't replace Harland," Lace Parasol informed Patrick.

"Harland is an angel up above," Bird Bonnet agreed. "And Deborah, an angel on earth."

Patrick certainly could not compete with that— not that he had any intention of trying. He admitted to liking Mrs. Cartwright more than he ought. He was relieved she had dismissed the idea to spend more time together.

A flirtation was unnecessary and messy. By the time Patrick returned to Brighton for the construction phase, she wouldn't be working at the inn any longer, anyway.

And it was not Mrs. Cartwright he wished to woo, but Salt&Sea. If their connection in person was anything like what it was on paper, Patrick actually *might* fall in love at first sight.

By then, thanks to his increase in wages and shares in the new gambling venture, Patrick could spoil Salt&Sea to her heart's desire. Take her anywhere she wished to go. Live happily ever after.

That was the only thing he should focus on.

Not some pretty proprietress—er, apparently a literal siren—to whom Patrick could bring nothing but disappointment and displeasure. In fact, he should do well to stay away from Mrs. Cartwright for the rest of his time here. For the foreseeable future, he would take care to—

"Mr. Gretham!" a lyrical voice called out.

He turned. Mrs. Cartwright hurried in their direction. Patrick's breath caught at her beauty. Her dark brown hair was pulled back beneath a fetching bonnet, leaving only a few soft tendrils to frame her face. The wind whipped her emerald-green walking dress behind her, outlining her form before blurring and billowing anew.

"Don't you start with the cow eyes," Bird Bonnet muttered in warning.

"Angel on earth," Lace Parasol reminded him. "Too good for the likes of you."

He took off his hat. "Mrs. Cartwright, I did not expect to see you today. May I be of service?"

"No, no." The wind brought high color to her cheeks. "It is I who can be of service. I shall be honored to give you the tour of Brighton you requested."

"Mm-hm," Lace Parasol murmured. "I knew he was up to no good."

"*Moo*," Bird Bonnet whispered.

He had no choice but to accept. As a gentleman. As a man of business. As a cow-eyed romantic fool who ought to know better than to tempt fate.

"It would be my absolute pleasure." Patrick held out his elbow to Mrs. Cartwright. "I have all day."

CHAPTER 8

*D*eborah stared at Mr. Gretham's outstretched arm. Then up over his well-tailored shoulders to the two bright-eyed busybodies, eager to take any semblance of gossip straight to the nearest drawing room. Then she swung her gaze back to Mr. Gretham's strong, waiting arm.

This was silly. Even for Brighton—haven of performed respectability—there was no reason to hesitate. Her ridiculous indecision was the only reason this moment now looked like A Moment.

They weren't doing anything *wrong*. She was doing something *right*. Deborah was away from her post, clothed in her best bonnet and walking dress, with the noble and necessary aim of saving Siren's Retreat.

Not…to spend the day with a man. Who was not her husband. And who was looking at her in increased confusion, but had not yet lowered his offered arm.

Just because it was her first outing with a man since her husband's sudden death five years ago, did not make it *An Outing With A Man*. Just because in all the years since, she had never taken a day—or even *half* a day—fully to herself for pleasure, did not make this *A Holiday*. Or *Shirking Her Duties*.

Saving her inn *was* her duty.

She hooked her gloved hand through the crook of Mr. Gretham's inner elbow and made a pleasant, but dismissive smile at the two busybodies avidly watching her every move.

"Have a lovely day, Mrs. Lennox and Mrs. Bates."

The two women sent each other looks of consternation. As much as they wanted to hang on like lichen, politeness dictated they take a step back and allow Deborah and her prospective future client to continue their day.

Inexplicably, Mrs. Bates seemed to *moo* lightly under her breath.

"Where shall we begin?" Mr. Gretham asked as soon as they were alone.

Not alone. Absolutely *not* alone. Standing on a pedestrian pavement on a very public road in a tourist-filled town.

It was just… Spending the day—or even a few hours—arm-in-arm with a handsome, charming man didn't *feel* like work. It felt like *fun*. Which made it feel right and disloyal all at the same time.

Deborah *was* Siren's Retreat. The inn was the

only baby she and her husband had ever shared. They'd poured every minute of their time into their creation, making the inn what it was today. Building the legend of True Love, side by side.

Should a woman with that history even notice the firm muscles beneath Mr. Gretham's frock coat? What about the width of his strong shoulders? His gorgeous hazel eyes? The way his hat crushed his soft brown curls to his forehead, giving a rumpled, boyish touch to his otherwise impeccable appearance?

These were treacherous waters.

Her correspondence with LostInLondon was safe because it was a *secret*. No one need know. There was nothing *to* know. As long as they never met, their connection would never go beyond the scrape of a plume on paper.

But if Deborah developed a temporary infatuation with an actual, living-and-breathing man, it would be disastrous on every count. Not just disloyal to Harland and what they had built together. A public flirtation would destroy the One True Love legend she'd spent years cultivating.

Not just cultivating...*believing*. Celebrating. *Selling*.

If her "Love Of A Lifetime" ended up looking like "Love For A Little While", what would happen to Siren's Retreat then?

People came in search of forever. In search of *eternal* love, as promised by the romantic love story of the proprietress herself. She *couldn't* look at

ERICA RIDLEY

another man. Stepping away from the registration counter was *dangerous*.

And yet, this was her best chance to save Siren's Retreat...and herself.

"We'll begin at the sea," she answered as lightly as she could. "The healing waters are the primary reason most visitors come to Brighton." Well...that, and social opportunities. Like the marriage mart. "You'll see that Siren's Retreat is uniquely situated to offer the perfect stroll to the gentlemen's beach or the ladies' beach, or the beautiful pedestrian promenade where I'm taking you now. Have you ever seen a finer view?"

"I have not," he replied.

Those were the right words. Deborah pretended not to notice he'd spoken them without lifting his gaze from her face. She could not help but blush.

The trick was to concentrate on the prize: an overpriced reservation—no, not overpriced, the *new* price—which could cover the unexpected leap in her own lease. That was all.

She and Mr. Gretham were both here for business purposes only. She needed to raise funds before the end of the month, and Mr. Gretham's employer was eager to spend money. Theirs was a perfect match, if of a different sort than the usual.

Deborah cleared her throat. "The two best suites at Siren's Retreat are on the second floor of each wing. They both have magnificent views from every window."

72

Mr. Gretham's hazel gaze seemed to sharpen. "Are both available?"

"They will be." Thank heavens. There was still time to raise prices. "Every room is reserved for this season, which has barely started. Many openings remain for next year."

He looked relieved to hear it.

Her heart beat faster. Perhaps this was a sign his employer had a larger party than she had presumed, and was hoping to secure multiple suites for his family and retinue.

"If you were to reserve now," she said as casually as she could, "I could offer the best rooms at a monthly price of…"

She named a fee so exorbitant that she could scarcely choke the words from her mouth. But at least this way, she had room to negotiate. She could lower the number by five percent, possibly even ten or fifteen, and still have enough to—

Mr. Gretham nodded. "That seems reasonable."

It *did?*

Her tight shoulders lightened with joy and hope. If she could deposit that sum into the inn's banking account before June, she could renew her lease. The money would give her a buffer to find more guests like Mr. Gretham's employer. She could possibly even start to *save* money, in the event Stanley decided to increase rents again five years from now. She wouldn't have enough money to buy the property outright, but at least she would be in no danger of losing her inn.

Deborah's fingers curled tighter around Mr. Gretham's arm, and she beamed at him. Taking him to the promenade was the absolute best use of her day—even if it *had* meant leaving Nancy in charge back at the inn.

And…it *was* nice to feel the cold wind buffeting against her bonnet. To feel hope in her chest. To stretch her legs, and fight the urge to give a little skip of excitement. Next season would be the best yet. She could feel it.

"Is anyone in your employer's party artistic?"

Mr. Gretham's gaze locked on hers. "Are *you* artistic?"

"Oh, that's not why I'm asking." She laughed and gestured at stretch of wet sand where waves lapped against the beach. "Many young ladies collect shells or even the seaweed and make imaginative creations out of it."

He cocked his head at the sand with obvious skepticism. "Seaweed sculptures?"

"Seaweed paintings," she clarified. "I have one in my parlor, as do many residents of Brighton. They're very cunning. Instead of brush strokes, the seaweed itself creates the art."

"Did you make the one in your parlor?"

She shook her head. "Not my forte."

His eyes snapped to attention. "What *is* your forte?"

"I sing a little," she hedged.

His lips parted. "I knew it!"

"You could tell by looking at me?" she asked in amusement.

"I could tell by listening to you. You have one of the most unique voices I've ever heard. It sounds like music, no matter what syllables you're saying. Do you sing professionally?"

"I used to," she admitted after a long moment, then mumbled, "Soprano, in the opera."

He stared in astonishment. "Never say you're ashamed to have such a wonderful talent!"

"Not at all," she assured him. "I love to sing. But some people make...certain assumptions...about women who perform on stage."

"I assume they're talented," he informed her. "No one has ever invited *me* on stage, which is the wisest choice for all involved. They protect their eardrums from rupture, and I protect my cravat from rotten tomatoes. Did you ever perform anywhere in London?"

"Everywhere in London. I used to tour England, which is how I ended up in Brighton. I met my husband after one of my performances. Harland had just heard me sing. He cornered me behind the curtain afterwards with such fervor, I thought he was going to propose an illicit arrangement. Instead, he proposed marriage." She smiled at the memory. "We held our wedding breakfast in what is now Siren's Retreat."

He reared back in horror. "You gave up a promising career as the main attraction in an opera with national acclaim...for a man?"

"I didn't 'give up,'" Deborah protested defensively, although she had in fact quit the opera that same night. "And it wasn't just 'for a man.' I chose *love*. Siren's Retreat—"

"—is not the opera. Your stage has shrunk to a three-foot by six-foot space behind a wooden counter. Your audience is now whomever pauses long enough to make a reservation or sign the registry."

"That's a horrid interpretation of my life." She gestured at the sand and sea around them. "I'm not at Siren's Retreat now, am I? I give tours on occasion. I don't live in a box."

"Don't you? How 'occasionally' do you offer tours? Before today, when was the last time you escaped your box for more than an hour or two?"

She crossed her arms and glared at him. There was nothing truthful she could say to refute his unsolicited observations.

"I don't mean to judge," he said, his voice soft.

"You're judging," she said flatly.

"I'm definitely judging," he agreed. "I just don't *mean* to. If you tell me giving up your love of singing professionally was the right decision for you, and that you never once regretted trading that life for this one…I'll believe you."

She rubbed her arms. "How can anyone know, at the moment of making a life-changing decision, whether they're making the right one? Any choice inherently means not choosing the other option. No matter which path you take, it would be perfectly normal for a small, fanciful part of you to occasionally *wonder...*"

"It's not too late. You're young. The opera—"

"It's definitely too late. I'm thirty-five. The opera was fifteen years ago and firmly in my past. Siren's Retreat is my present."

"It doesn't sound like a present to me. It sounds like a lot of work for less fame and fortune. If you suddenly found yourself with unexpected time on your hands, I should hope that you would consider the possibility resuming your dreams and doing something active with your talent."

"As you correctly—and infuriatingly—pointed out," she said dryly, "I never have free time on my hands."

"But if you did," he insisted. "Your life wouldn't be over. It would simply be the beginning of a new act."

She tilted her head and considered him. He seemed oddly passionate about her happiness and well-being. As if he wanted to be certain that no matter what happened, she would thrive.

But why should he think otherwise? She *was* thriving here in Brighton. Siren's Retreat was a popular destination—and soon to be more financially sound than ever.

Perhaps he was the sort of person who was so dazzled by any sort of celebrity that he could not imagine choosing something as personal as love over something as impersonal as a faceless, ever-changing audience.

Or perhaps he was a kindhearted gentleman with an overly sympathetic soul, and the thought of Deborah walking away from her first dream made him fear she had not found joy in all the new dreams that followed.

"I'm truly happy," she assured him. "Siren's Retreat is my life, and it is a *good* life. I wouldn't wish to do anything else, or to be anywhere else. I wake up every morning grateful that this is the path I chose. It's the right one for me."

He did not look assuaged by her assurances. "Mrs. Cartwright—"

"Deborah," she corrected with a chuckle. "If I am to be baring my heart to you."

"Patrick." He took her hands in his and held them tight. "I have no right—none at all—"

She waited, but he said nothing more. Just gripped her hands and stared at her beseechingly, belligerently, besottedly. As if he were confused and angry and half in love all at the same time and would rather not be any of it.

Deborah wanted him to see she had no such anguish. She was very happy—very!—with no regrets at all, none, not for a single moment. She certainly was not plagued by sudden indecision or fighting unexpected amorous impulses. Not for her dearest LostInLondon, and certainly not for handsome Mr. Gretham...er, *Patrick*...whom she'd first-named in a fit of...

Nothing. Deborah didn't have fits of any kind. Her world was steady, predictable, unchanging.

Fulfilling. Her life was already one hundred percent fulfilling. Yes, she'd started a correspondence with a total stranger, whose friendship had become the most important relationship in her life. But that was pure happenstance. And anonymous. They could put their plumes down and walk away at any time.

As for walking away at any time from the earnest gentlemen standing right before her... well, that was a little trickier. In part because her hands were clutched in his. Possibly clutching him right back.

Which, again, was not *romantic* in any way. This long, leisurely stroll along the most picturesque beach in all of Brighton contained no *hidden meaning.*

She was just a humble proprietress on the hunt for a big fish in order to pay her rent. And Patrick was the big fish. Or at least, the medium-sized fish who worked for the bigger fish. This was business, not pleasure. He was searching for the best spot to holiday, and she was showing him that he'd already found it. They were performing their respective professional duties, not engaging in an extremely unwise (and impossible, given Deborah already found her true love) flirtation.

None of which explained why he had taken her hands in his so passionately.

Or why she had *left* them there, to be caressed gently by the pads of his thumbs. As if he were just as resistant to romance—and just as powerless to stop himself.

"Deborah," he said softly.

His eyes were heavy-lidded and unblinking. Drinking her in, as if her face was the elixir of life. As though he were thinking about kissing her. As if she might let him.

He leaned closer. *Definitely* considering kissing her. And clearly unsure if she would let him—or if it was a wise decision, even if both parties were willing.

Which she wasn't. She'd had and lost the only man for her. There was no replacing Harland, and no reason to waste time with men who were not him. She'd known when they met that she'd never know love like that again. Just as she'd known at the funeral that her arms would never again hold a partner tight in an embrace. That her lips would never again kiss, or be kissed.

All of which was why she was going to put Patrick in his place right this second. Before he got any further ideas. Before he *tried* something.

Before she stood here and let him.

Just to see. Just to know. Just to *feel*.

"Deborah?" came a disbelieving voice from the promenade behind them. "Is that you?"

The parson.

With a gasp, she jerked her fingers from Patrick's hands. She placed her palms to her heart to calm the storm within, and backed away from him, limbs shaking.

"Mrs. Cartwright," she told him. Even her voice trembled. The one thing she'd always had full control over. "I bid you good day, Mr. Gretham. Come and see me when you are serious about making a reservation."

Patrick winced. "Deb—That is, Mrs.—"

But she had already turned away and was running across the promenade, past the startled gazes of locals and tourists alike, hurrying away from temptation. Away from *him*.

Away from what might have been.

CHAPTER 9

*P*atrick did not return to Siren's Retreat.
At least, not inside.

He had another stroll about the perimeter and made a few more notes in his journal before being overcome by the creeping sensation of how visible he was from the inn's many windows, and what Deborah—Mrs. Cartwright, rather—might think if she glimpsed him casually jotting notes on the other side of the pavement.

These were not the only reasons he was avoiding Siren's Retreat. *Avoiding* was the wrong word. Avoiding implied he *ought* to be there, when really, he had no reason to be. He'd arrived in Brighton in possession of months of research painstakingly culled from guidebooks and inter-views and letters. One could never develop *too* excellent a bargaining position, but really, with Lord Edgewick's bottomless purse at Patrick's disposal, the conclusion had never been in any doubt.

All Patrick had to do was make the offer. That was it. The entirety of his lines would be something like, "How much gold would you like to have? Splendid! Hold out your hands and I'll count it out. There you go, that's a good man. Hand over the deed and I'll be on my way."

It would be the swiftest and easiest negotiation ever transacted.

So why hadn't he completed it yet?

He was not ready to admit that part of the answer was Deborah. Patrick wasn't usually one to hide from the truth. He knew exactly who he was and what he was up to.

None of which was supposed to involve seducing a widow on a public pier.

Definitely not the widow related to the owner of the land he was meant to be buying. If Patrick insisted on engaging in ill-advised scandalous behavior, the prudent time to do so was *after* the property transfer had been made.

Not that he was here to indulge in any scandalous behavior! Well, all right, that had been a large part of his plans. But not with Deborah. Patrick had been hoping to forge a lasting connection with a completely different woman. He was here for Salt&Sea, who had never once mentioned still being in love with a dead man or believing that every person only ever got one opportunity for happiness.

That was the woman whom Fate was supposed to bring into his life. Salt&Sea *enjoyed* their connection, wanted it, sought him out. Opened up to him on purpose. If such a thing as soulmates existed, *she* was the closest Patrick had ever found. Not Deborah.

So he did the only thing that he could:

He wrote to Salt&Sea telling her he'd spend the next few days visiting each of the spots she'd mentioned in her letters, starting with her favorites. If there was such a thing as "meant to be", then their paths should collide.

And if Salt&Sea would rather not risk stumbling across him face-to-face... Well, then he supposed she'd stay at home until after he was gone. But at least he would have tried.

Patrick glanced up at the sign overhead. Sharp's Tea Room. This location was mentioned twice as often as any other in her letters, and was therefore Destiny's best chance at tossing the correspondents together.

He curled his gloved hand around the iron door handle and glanced up at the clear skies overhead.

"I'm ready," he informed Destiny. Or tempted Fate. Whichever gods were listening. "Show me some divine intervention."

With that, he took a deep breath and opened the door.

Music spilled out of the café. Sound flowed over him and around him like water, as if he'd opened a secret door to Atlantis in the middle of the sea.

Much of the music came from a pianoforte in the center of the tea room, but the best part, the most powerful part, the waves and the whirlwind and the great frothing ripples that danced and glittered everywhere, floated out from the lungs of none other than Mrs. Deborah Cartwright.

He stared at her, speechless. Incapable of taking a single step. Of doing anything at all besides blocking the doorway like a human statue. Frozen in place on the outside, but with every fiber of his being on the inside alive and roaring, as if suddenly set free.

The other patrons sent no pointed looks at him for his strange behavior and awkward presence, hulking in the doorway. They hadn't noticed him at all. He could have entered the tea room balancing on his hands, juggling baby jaguars with his feet, and no one would have noticed a thing.

They were all staring slack-jawed, just like him, at the spectacle they'd apparently known to expect. Every chair contained a spellbound patron, and every table a completely untouched cup of tea, utterly forgotten in the presence of such wondrous, auditory magic.

Siren's Retreat, indeed. It wasn't just a catchy name. It was *her* name, *her* essence. Her voice, the web from which it was impossible to escape, because no escape would be sought. To hear her soaring soprano was to feel each syllable in his bones, in his blood, in his soul.

Each note danced along his skin, kissing him

like a crisp sea breeze on a sweltering summer's day. He wanted to bask in it forever. To lay down right there at her feet, close his eyes, and let her voice transport him anywhere she pleased.

He was wrong. Lace Parasol and Bird Bonnet were right.

Some legends were true.

When the song ended, a sluggish beat passed in silence as the room collectively roused itself from its enchanted slumber before erupting into a round of enthusiastic applause. Many patrons rose to their feet, giving Deborah and the pianist a well-deserved standing ovation.

Patrick was still on his feet, grinning as wide and clapping as loud as everyone else in the audience. It took a while to remember what he had come for. Er, *who* he had come for. Not a surprisingly phenomenal show—or even the increasingly *un*surprisingly phenomenal Deborah Cartwright—but in hope of meeting Salt&Sea.

After spending less than five minutes in Sharp's Tea Room, Patrick fully understood why his friend adored it above all others. He would be delighted to visit with her, a dozen times a day if it pleased her.

He scanned the audience in search of her face. Complicated, of course, by the fact that he didn't know what Salt&Sea's countenance *looked* like. A mix of logic and romantic optimism allowed him to make some inferences.

No one below the age of twenty, surely. Make that twenty-five. She knew too much about the town and wrote her letters with too much maturity to be a green miss fresh from the schoolroom.

Likewise, not any of the women obviously here with children or their husbands. Salt&Sea had never *mentioned* a family, so Patrick had decided that she, like him, did not have one. That they might become a family together. Certainly their letters had crossed the line from friendliness and into flirtation on more than one occasion. She had never *said* so, not outright, but from the very first letter, Patrick had the impression Salt&Sea was just as lonely as he was.

None of the spectators present matched the fantasy in his mind, however. None were alone, for one. They all had husbands or children or a gaggle of friends crowded about the table with them. None was a conspicuously single woman seated alone with a large writing slope atop her tea table, along with a plume and ink and a tall stack of his old letters.

But he *did* spy one small, vacant table, barely big enough for two, tucked into the farthest corner of the tea room.

Quickly, he stepped away from the door and made his way to the empty chair before someone else could come into the tea room and beat him to the only remaining seat.

A dark-haired man in an apron so covered in colorful foodstuffs that it appeared paint-splattered rushed out from the kitchen and over to the pianoforte. He pulled the pianist to her feet and planted a kiss on her upturned face with such flair and obvious pride that this, too, was greeted with a round of delighted applause, rather than gasps of shock at such scandalous behavior.

While the happy couple was busy staring into each other's eyes and smiling giddily, Deborah stepped away from the pianoforte. Or tried to. She could barely take more than a single step at a time because everyone wanted to wish her well and thank her for her performance.

Now that he'd heard her sing, Patrick wasn't entirely certain he could speak to her at all without stammering like a schoolboy. Not that he expected her to stop at his table. *Un*-first-naming him and running off had been fairly clear clues indicating her disinterest in forming any sort of relationship with him.

Not that he was interested in a liaison! Well, all right, he *was*, which was the devil of it. He'd developed feelings for Salt&Sea, come to Brighton in hopes of making their epistolary correspondence an in-person *affaire de cœur*, but now that he was here, the one woman he could not keep from his mind was Deborah Cartwright.

It was a good thing the pretty proprietress was not seeking a man, Patrick reminded himself. Least of all, him. Circumstances would soon reveal him to be her enemy. Enemy-by-proxy, if one wished to be technical about it. He was turning her sweet inn into a debauched gaming hell on the earl's orders, not Patrick's own whim.

Nonetheless, he doubted Deborah would appreciate the distinction.

He started in surprise when she slid into the chair across from him at the tiny table, and then realized she'd had no choice, since it was the only empty seat in the tea room. In fact, given how crowded the tea room was…

He winced. "Tell me I'm not in your chair."

She pantomimed sewing her lips closed.

Of course he was. "I didn't realize because… I was so… You were so…" He splayed his hands on the table, preparing to push himself to his feet. "I'll go."

She placed her hand atop his. "Stay."

He tried not to look at her bare fingers crossed over his, though he could not help but feel their warmth and softness. He wondered if the rest of her was as soft and warm. If her curves would feel as sweet pressed against him. If her lips would taste as intoxicating as her song.

He cleared his throat because he could not clear his mind. "I saw part of your performance. Heard, rather. You were marvelous."

She withdrew her hand from his.

The loss echoed through him. He longed to reach for both of her hands. To cradle them in his, to caress their soft skin just as he yearned to caress every bit of her—but of course, such thoughts would not do. He tried his best to think of her as a distant acquaintance. A beautiful, talented stranger who, thanks to his own employer, would soon be out of a home and a post...

"Thank you." She was obviously used to compliments, had weathered twenty minutes of effusive praise in the short distance from the stage to her seat, and yet twin blooms of color blossomed high on her cheeks.

The aproned man who had kissed the pianist arrived with tea service for two and began to arrange it on the table.

"Oh, no." Patrick straightened, afraid he'd inadvertently been even more presumptuous than he'd feared. "I did not order—"

"It's on the house," the man said. "For Mrs. Cartwright and guest."

Patrick was hardly here as her invited guest, but Deborah did not correct the man, and the tea service looked splendid.

A loud crash echoed in another room. The dark-haired man sprinted toward the kitchen without delay.

"That was John Sharp," Deborah explained. "The chef behind Sharp's Tea Room."

"Ah. The pianist is his wife?"

"Yes. John and Allegra met whilst staying at Siren's Retreat on holiday," she said with obvious pride.

More pride, in fact, than the dutiful smiles she'd given in response to the crowd's effusive praise of her incredible voice. There was nothing Deborah valued more than Siren's Retreat.

Patrick swallowed. The delicious tea service now tasted like dust.

"You're a bachelor," she said. "Perhaps when you visit with your employer, you too might find love."

He shook his head. There would *be* no Siren's Retreat on his next visit. Not that he was at liberty to say so, until the contracts were signed and the deed in his employer's hand.

But Deborah appeared to be waiting for Patrick to say *something.*

"I...already have someone in mind," he blurted out.

A flurry of emotions crossed her face before she could school her countenance back into a blank expression. Into her proprietress face, he realized. Calm, pleasant, professional, impersonal. A mask.

"My felicitations to the lucky lady," she said lightly.

This made him sound like even more of a cad than he would have seemed if he would have grabbed her hands and caressed them the way he'd wanted to.

She'd *known* he wanted to touch her. And now she knew he was also involved with someone else.

"I'm not promised," he tried to explain. "In fact, we've not even—"

"I'm married to Siren's Retreat," she interrupted. A pronouncement which did nothing to ease his creeping sense of guilt. "But there's no competition. Wherever you find love is by default the perfect place to find it."

Of course life was a competition. A woman did not become a famed soprano with top billing on tour across the country by *not* competing for her rightful space. She'd traded her voice for an inn, but the game had not changed. Brighton was the new stage. Of all its sundry hostelry, Siren's Retreat was the star. Instead of touring England, England now came rushing to Deborah's door.

And Patrick—Patrick who had admired her hands, and her voice, and her brain, Patrick who had almost kissed her when given half a chance, despite allegedly professing interest in another woman—was here to take it all away from her.

Married to it, she'd said. Deborah had not chosen that word by accident. She was reminding him that her heart was promised elsewhere, too. She was still in love with her dead husband and just as enamored of every beam and stone in her inn. She wasn't just helping others find the happiness she had known, but also holding on to her belief in one single eternal love, whose bond Death itself could never break.

And certainly not an ordinary man of business like Patrick.

"I should go," she said. "I've been away from my inn for too long."

"May I walk you to your door, Mrs. Cartwright?"

"That depends." Her tone was light, teasing, but her eyes were serious. "Are your intentions chaste?"

"No," he answered honestly.

She blinked. It was impossible to say whether she was shocked by the answer itself or his willingness to own up to it. "Then I should say no, as well, Mr. Gretham."

"Probably," he agreed. "Though the offer still stands."

She chewed on her lower lip. "It's a short walk. A *public* walk. We wouldn't be alone together, not really."

"I promise not to kiss you," he offered. "Unless you ask me to."

Her eyebrows shot up in amusement. "And then you would, but only because it would be impolite for a gentleman not to give a lady anything she desires?"

"That would be one reason, yes. But mostly because when I look at you, I—"

"Oh, don't tell me." Her cheeks flushed pink. "Since there's no future in it, what does it matter? We'll walk together and say goodbye and that will be the end."

Yet it felt like their time together *did* matter. Like they *could* have a future. If they both agreed to a slightly different future than the one they had envisioned for themselves up until a fortnight ago.

He offered her his arm and waited until they were outside before asking, "What if tonight wasn't the end of it? Of us?"

She glanced at him sharply. Or tried to. But the color in her cheeks was high again. Wind whipped the light tendrils framing her face in every direction, making her seem more approachable than ever.

More kissable.

Patrick berated himself for noticing, for getting lost in her beauty, but it was no use. If he closed his eyes, he would still be swept away by the ethereal sound of her voice. Undone by the softness of her skin and the scent of her hair.

"Do you mean," she said carefully, "that we will necessarily see each other again during your employer's future holiday at Siren's Retreat?"

"I have not said—" he began.

"You have not said," she agreed, her eyes twinkling, "but I am afraid there is no mystery. Siren's Retreat *is* the best Brighton has to offer. If you are holding back from securing a reservation because you think I'll no longer deign to speak to you once the transaction is guaranteed, let me assure you I will not treat you any differently."

Patrick had never wanted to kiss her more than in this moment. To show her without words how much he liked her. What he wished they could have. How well they could fit together.

He held his tongue, in part because of his duty to his employer...and the probable reaction the news of the planned gaming hell would bring.

But also, he could not speak from the heart because it would be unfair to the woman he had *thought* he had come to Brighton to meet. Honor dictated that his first allegiance was to Salt&Sea. There was no official understanding between them, but Patrick could not begin a romance with anyone else without at least attempting to meet Salt&Sea first.

No matter which directions his heart tugged.

He paused just before the walkway to Siren's Retreat. "Mrs. Cartwright—"

"Deborah." She sent him an embarrassed look up through her lashes. "I apologize for yesterday. I did not run away because I dislike you, but because I *do*. It's...complicated."

"I like you, too," was all he could admit for now. "It *is* complicated. More so than one might think. Will you be singing at Sharp's Tea Room tomorrow?"

She shook her head. "I try to leave Nancy alone as little as possible. In fact, I ought to see what scrapes she's managed to get into in the hour I was away. And you? How shall you spend the afternoon?"

"Trying to extricate myself from a few scrapes of my own."

CHAPTER 10

The letter was waiting for him when Patrick checked his post.

He meant to return to his hotel and read the response in the privacy of his guest chamber, but he barely managed three steps out the door before backing against the cobble-fronted façade of the post office to tear open the wax seal of Salt&Sea's latest letter.

Once it was in his hands, however, he hesitated before reading her words. He had come to Brighton in search of Salt&Sea. This was it. Her reply would determine what path came next. If she wished to meet even half as ardently, then his search was over. He would squash his interest in Deborah and give one hundred percent of his attention and effort to Salt&Sea.

Any woman he wooed deserved no less than his all.

My dearest Lost In London,

Please do not despise me for what I say next. I have enjoyed our correspondence more than I can express. I did not even know I needed you, and then there you were, on the other side of a pen. I was the one who was lost until you found me, and showed me I was only living half a life. In describing my surroundings to you, I saw them anew with fresh eyes. I appreciate where and who I am in a way that I hadn't in years, thanks to you.

Part of the reason I have been able to bare my soul —or perhaps, the entire reason—is because of our anonymity. I know the wonderful, witty, kindhearted, thoughtful person you are on the inside. My imagination is more than capable of providing the rest.

We have created a paradox together, by showing our true selves while hiding everything else. I fear real life can never live up to the fantasy we've built, on either side. I do not wish to ruin our friendship by introducing awkwardness and stiff conversation where before there was none.

And that is all this can be: friendship. Despite never having met you, despite knowing we never will meet, I nonetheless consider you one of my dearest friends, and hope we remain so, for as long as we can hold a pen in our gnarled hands.

Yours as always,

Salt & Sea

WELL.

Patrick read the letter a second time, then a third, not quite able to decipher the jumble of feelings in his chest.

Was he disappointed Salt&Sea rejected his invitation to meet in person to explore a possible romance? Yes. But…not nearly as disappointed as he would have expected himself to be on the drive up from London, when he was dreaming about coming face-to-face with her.

She was right. The woman he'd been half in love with was a fantasy, or at least partially so. He knew her in every way that *mattered*; he knew her heart, her mind, her hopes. The rest had indeed been supplied by his imagination.

There was a very real possibility of their first glimpse of each other bringing disappointment. Of the words, which flowed so easily on paper when one could take one's time to craft the perfect sentence, to become awkward and stilted. To discover they were not two halves of a whole after all, but just two lonely people whose letters had happened to cross paths at just the right time.

Salt&Sea was a fantasy.

Mrs. Deborah Cartwright was *real*.

Patrick identified the strange emotion in his chest: relief. He was *relieved* Salt&Sea had gently rejected his invitation. As fond as he was of his correspondent, his thoughts had been full of Deborah from the moment they first met. He could now let go of the guilt those feelings had brought.

He was not betraying Salt&Sea. He was free to pursue happiness wherever he found it.

Wooing Deborah held its own complications. She would not be pleased to see the Earl of Edgewick turn her inn into a gaming hell. But she needn't watch it happen.

Once Patrick received his shares in the new venture and the increased wages, he could afford to take her anywhere she wished. They could live a life of leisure if she wanted. And if what she wanted was to return to the stage and perform before crowds of thousands, he fully supported that, too.

And if what she wants is Siren's Retreat? a nagging voice asked at the back of his mind.

Oh, if only that was something he could offer! It was not fear of losing a flirtation that tied his hands, but the threat of losing his post, his security, his hard-won future. A chill fluttered across Patrick's skin. He had to return with a deed in hand. *At any cost*, the earl had said.

Deborah might be that cost.

But must she be?

What if there *was* an alternate location here in Brighton that would serve just as well for the earl's needs...without destroying a beloved tourist destination, and life as she knew it?

CHAPTER 11

*W*hen the front door to Siren's Retreat swung open, Deborah was showing Nancy how to mark the reservation calendar to hold specific dates for potential customers. Deborah glanced up from the book, hoping the interruption was a certain broad-shouldered gentleman with silver-brown hair and warm hazel eyes.

It was not.

Her busybody neighbors, Mrs. Lennox and Mrs. Bates, swept into the inn like the high winds of a tempest.

"Is it true?" Mrs. Bates barked from beneath her wide-brimmed bonnet.

Deborah closed the calendar book. "Is what true?"

Mrs. Lennox shook out her parasol over the reception area's previously pristine floor. "That you're thinking of selling this place."

Deborah gasped. "I could never!"

"She could never," Nancy agreed. "Aunt Cartwright doesn't own this land. My father does."

A distinction that only served to unsettle Deborah's stomach further.

Stanley had *promised* to let her renew her lease… as long as she could pay the higher rent, or prove Siren's Retreat was worth keeping at any price. Thus far, she was not any closer to meeting either objective. But how would her neighbors know?

Frivolous rumors about Siren's Retreat closing down or being handed off to new management would destroy any hope of filling the reservation book…and render Deborah incapable of meeting the new rents, ensuring her brother-in-law the freedom to sell the property at will. Yet she could not imagine Stanley gossiping about family matters with outsiders.

She placed her elbows on the counter and leaned forward. "Why do you ask?"

Mrs. Lennox and Mrs. Bates looked thrilled to be in possession of information that was not yet common knowledge.

"Why, because of the investor going 'round town, tempting every venue in sight with promises of boundless gold, if only they can prove *their* location superior to this one."

Deborah bit back a groan. If this was true, then the mystery investor had already all but decided to purchase her property. *Stanley Cartwright's* property, rather. How could she possibly convince her brother-in-law that Siren's Retreat was worth more than boundless gold?

If the rumor was true.

She narrowed her eyes. "What investor?"

Mrs. Lennox and Mrs. Bates exchanged reluctant glances. "We didn't catch his name."

"Did you *see* this investor? With your own eyes?"

"We heard about him," Mrs. Lennox admitted.

"From several reputable sources," Mrs. Bates added quickly.

"Like the time you were certain Napoleon Bonaparte had escaped his exile in Elba only to be hiding in one of the bathing machines right here in Brighton?"

"It's a very nice beach," Mrs. Lennox said stiffly.

"Better than Elba," Mrs. Bates added. "Italians don't even *use* bathing machines."

"Do French people?" Nancy asked.

"Napoleon and his wife are very fashionable," Mrs. Bates assured her. "He would do as is genteel."

Deborah raised a brow. "Such as...declare himself emperor and invade half of Europe, waging war on—"

"He wasn't in the bathing machine after all," Mrs. Lennox interrupted. "And really, that misidentification has nothing at all to do with—"

"—the alleged investor you've not actually identified?" Deborah finished.

"Maybe it's Napoleon," Nancy said helpfully.

"It's not Napoleon," Mrs. Lennox said in exasperation.

"It *could* be," Mrs. Bates countered dreamily. "He's already escaped once, and Brighton *does* have nice beaches. If anyone could put his hands on boundless gold, surely we agree that Napoleon Bonaparte—"

The door swung open again.

"Please don't be Napoleon," Deborah muttered.

"*Worse*," Mrs. Lennox stage-whispered. "It's that too-forward Town gentleman who's always making moo-eyes at you."

Deborah snapped up straight. She tucked a wayward tendril behind her ear just as Patrick stepped into the room. He held a small brown paper package in one hand and a quizzical expression upon his face.

His hazel eyes met hers. "Is this a bad time to call?"

"Ha!" Mrs. Bates crowed. "He admits he's a *gentleman caller*."

"Everyone who calls on someone else is a caller," Nancy pointed out. "The two of you are *lady* callers."

Mrs. Lennox lifted her chin. "But we are not the sort of individuals who—"

"—paid for a guided tour of the exterior grounds?" Deborah held up the reservation book, which contained no such reservation. "Of course I am ready for our scheduled appointment, Mr. Gretham. Nancy, please mind the counter until I return. Mrs. Lennox, Mrs. Bates, lovely to see you, as always."

Before her sharp-eyed neighbors could do more than clap a pale hand to their bodices, Deborah ducked under the counter, wrapped her fingers about Patrick's free arm, and dragged him right back out the door.

"You forgot your bonnet!" Mrs. Lennox called out.

"People will talk!" Mrs. Bates' voice added.

"I'm scandalized," Patrick whispered as he jogged arm-in-arm to keep up with Deborah. "Should you wear my top hat, to be safe?"

"No hat can save me now." Laughing, Deborah ducked into a grove of elm trees and sank to the soft grass at the base of a large tree. It had been years since she'd last felt so young and free.

Patrick flopped down beside her, heedless of the ill effects bark and grass would have upon his expertly tailored clothing, and handed her the brown-paper package he'd been carrying. "Fancy a tea cake?"

"Always." She untied the string and folded down the edges of the paper to reveal her favorite cakes filling half the package, and a style she did not recognize on the other. "Are these...?"

"From Sharp's Tea Room? Yes. I asked the chef if he knew which cakes you might prefer."

"And John said, 'Deborah abhors change, and only ever orders one kind?'"

"He said...you hold a deep appreciation for tradition," Patrick hedged politely.

"Mm-hm. And these other cakes? I assume they're your favorites?"

"I've never tasted them before in my life," he said cheerfully. "They're all for you."

She lifted her brows. "Your gift includes cakes you already knew I wouldn't prefer?"

"I don't know that, and neither do you." His tone was light and teasing, but his gaze was oddly intense. "What if you do like this new kind more than the old cakes? Trying something new doesn't mean anything was wrong with the old way. It just means there might be more than one perfectly acceptable path to happiness."

Perhaps because Deborah *was* uncommonly happy, with her legs flung out in the dappled grass and her shoulders relaxed against the thick ridges of a tree trunk, and with Patrick at her side, she reached not for the comforting sameness of her usual lemon cakes, but the less familiar brown squares.

Why not? The past few months had been full of firsts. She'd hired her niece as her assistant, answered a few anonymous travel queries as a favor, begun a correspondence with her friend LostInLondon for the purely selfish reason of enjoying their conversations—

Her fingers paused with the new tea cake a few inches from her mouth. Once upon a time, she had imagined what it might be like to have moments like these with LostInLondon, only to push those thoughts away out of fear she was being disloyal to her late husband.

And now here she was—not in her daydreams, but in the flesh—seated next to an attractive man with no chaperonage whatsoever, engaged in exactly the sort of romantic tête-à-tête she'd sworn never to find herself in again.

More than that. She'd claimed it would be *impossible*.

The bond with one's true love was supposed to be eternal. That was what she was really selling, here at Siren's Retreat. Not a few weeks in a guest chamber, but forevermore with Destiny itself.

Wasn't that why she had declined LostInLondon's invitation to meet? Because they had grown too close, and she was terrified of putting her claims to the test?

Was there more than one perfectly acceptable path to happiness?

Patrick's handsome face filled with charming nervousness. "Is something wrong? Should I—"

She bit down on the tea cake to avoid responding.

Flavor exploded across her tongue. Honey and cinnamon and vanilla and nutmeg. The new tea cakes were *good*, damn him. Better than good. *Shove-them-into-my-mouth-by-the-handful* delicious. Wanton and decadent and dreadfully addictive.

His forehead lined with worry. "If you don't like them…"

She stuffed the rest of the tea cake into her mouth and moved the package out of his reach.

Delight infused his face. "You do like them!"

"Go and get more," she said with her mouth full.

"I don't think I will." He pretended to reach for one of the cakes. "I think I'll share these with you."

She slapped his hand away. "*My* cakes. You were very clear on this point. I'm afraid you must find your own path to happiness."

"Maybe I am." He held up clawed hands in a playful *I'm-going-to-get-you* pose. "Maybe my path to happiness is right here."

"Uh-uh." She shook her head, closing the brown paper wrapping for safety before letting her shoulders slide away from the trunk and fall to the ground, flinging the parcel well out of his reach.

He ignored the parcel and followed her instead, covering her body with his, right there on the grass. His hat tumbled from his head, but he didn't go after it. His eyes were on hers, his mouth mere inches away.

"There's a crumb on your upper lip." His voice was husky.

She slid the tip of her tongue out from her mouth and licked the crumb away.

"Rude," he murmured. "I wanted a taste."

Should she? Could she?

Her heart beat too fast, too loud. "Come and taste it, then."

Before she could regret the words, rescind the

invitation, his lips were on hers, opening her mouth, suckling her tongue.

She forgot all about the tea cakes. Her fingers threaded through his hair, pulling him to her. He rolled on the grass so that she was on top, setting the course, controlling the speed and depth of the kiss.

Diabolical. Now she could not blame him for taking advantage, could not pretend she'd been anything but an enthusiastic participant in a torrent of kisses hotter than white sand on a summer day. It was *her* bosom crushed against Patrick's chest. *Her* fingers twining in his hair, stroking the edge of his jaw. *Her* tongue, returning again and again to tangle with his.

Her defenses crumbling like the lightest tea cake.

Her beliefs and assumptions turned inside out and upside down.

"I have to go." Her words were breathy and unconvincing, even to her own ears. But his warm hands immediately lifted from the curve of her hips.

"If you must."

"I must," she assured him, assured herself, but it was another few heartbeats before she gathered enough willpower to peel herself from his lithe, strong body. "I left Nancy at the counter. Anything could happen."

"You're right," he said softly. "Anything could happen."

He wasn't talking about Nancy. He was saying *lie atop me again, and see what happens.* Lord knew,

Deborah's quickening body was eager to find out. She could not allow it.

She scrambled over to the abandoned tea cakes instead, holding the brown-paper package to her chest like a shield against temptation.

"I…" What? *I enjoyed kissing you? I want to keep kissing you? I will never be able to try another cake without remembering the taste of your mouth and the heat of your kisses?*

"Me, too."

He locked his fingers behind his head. As though he intended to stay sprawled here atop the grass all day and all night. In case Deborah turned up, hungry for more kisses.

There was nothing she could say. She turned and ran instead, telling herself her haste was due to her responsibilities as a proprietress… Not because she was too cowardly to continue the path she'd started all the way to its inevitable end.

When she burst through the front door of the inn, Mrs. Lennox and Mrs. Bates were gone from the reception area. Deborah's younger niece Sybil stood in their place.

"Oh, Aunt, there you are." Sybil picked at her fingernails, apparently finding more of concern there than in her aunt's disheveled hair and grass-stained gown. "I came as soon as I heard."

Deborah tied her package firmly before setting the tea cakes on the counter. "Heard what?"

"About the investor," Nancy said. "It's not Bonaparte."

Deborah stared at her nieces in momentary confusion. She'd forgotten all about the earlier gossip whilst distracted with Patrick's drugging kisses.

"Of course it isn't Napoleon Bonaparte." She turned to Sybil with a frown. "Why on earth would Mrs. Lennox and Mrs. Bates visit *you* to spread such gossip?"

Sybil blinked. "Who?"

"They didn't," Nancy said. "Sybil, tell her what you told me."

"I'm not *really* allowed in Father's study," Sybil stammered. "If I glimpsed papers I should not have, it's because they were out in the open, where anyone might stumble across them—"

"What papers?" Deborah grabbed her niece's hands. "Just tell me."

"Father's going to sell," Sybil blurted. "No matter what you do."

Deborah dropped her niece's hands, her ears buzzing. "What?"

"The inn won't be under new management." The words tumbled from Sybil's mouth in a blur. "There won't be an inn at all. They're going to knock it down and build a gaming hell. Right where we're standing."

"*What?*" Deborah's hip slumped against the counter. She splayed a hand atop its familiar scarred surface. Ran her other hand over the wallpaper she'd pasted on herself.

"That's not the important part," Nancy scolded her sister.

"How could anything be more important?" Deborah's voice was hollow. "Your father wishes to turn a haven into a hell. Where fortunes are lost and lives ruined, instead of love gained and lives transformed for the better."

"Not Father," Sybil said. "The investor is going to do that. An investor by the name of...."

Nancy gave up waiting on her sister to tell the whole story. "It's Mr. Gretham!"

What?

Deborah spun away from her nieces and raced back outside into the crisp spring air. If Patrick was still sprawled on the grass waiting for more kisses, he was about to get the surprise of his life when she smacked him with a tree branch instead.

He wasn't there.

Why should he be? He'd taken what he wanted.

She slammed the side of her fist against the tree, then rubbed her face with her hands. She couldn't compete with coffers of bottomless gold, just like she couldn't undo the kisses they had shared.

But she *could* prove she did not need him.

Maybe he was right. Maybe there *were* multiple paths to happiness. But her steps would never again lead her to a blackguard like him.

It was time to meet LostInLondon.

CHAPTER 12

*P*atrick glanced at his pocket watch and debated breaking into a light jog. If he didn't hurry, he would be late to his meeting with Stanley Cartwright. The one thing a skilled man of business never wished to begin negotiations with was a disadvantage.

But as close as Cartwright's residence was to Patrick's lodgings, the post office was even closer. Residual guilt had driven him through its doors. He had come to Brighton in hopes of pursuing a real-life romance with Salt&Sea, but had not thought of her once yesterday whilst flirting with Deborah. *Kissing* Deborah. Salt&Sea's newest letter now weighed down his pocket like lead.

Patrick glanced at his pocket watch and strode faster. There was no time. He would have to read it after his meeting.

It was good that Salt&Sea had declined his offer to meet in person. They could maintain an epistolary friendship, but Patrick now knew he wanted nothing more than that. Deborah had stolen his heart without even trying, and Patrick would do anything in his power to please her.

The problem was, the thing she wanted most was not in his power to grant.

He had spent the past week speaking to representatives of every major proprietor and landowner in town, desperate to discover an alternative even more splendid than Siren's Retreat.

There was none. Deborah was right. Her location was perfect in every way. The Earl of Edgewick was eager to begin. If Patrick did not return to London with the deed in hand, he would lose his post, the raise in salary, and the financial security for himself and his future wife, all in the space of a breath. What could he offer Deborah then?

If Patrick botched these negotiations on purpose, Stanley would simply sell to someone else. Patrick's noble sacrifice would leave him unemployed and prospect-less, and Deborah would lose her inn regardless. At least with Patrick's increased income and investment dividends, he could provide an easy, comfortable life. She need never again stand on her feet behind a wooden counter fifteen hours a day, seven days a week.

He hoped that would be enough.

After Patrick arrived at the Cartwright residence, the butler quickly ushered him straight back to the familiar study.

Stanley's eyes brightened at the sight of his

ERICA RIDLEY

conduit to gold. "Come in, come in. Help yourself to a nip of brandy."

Patrick declined the tipple and seated himself in a chair on the opposite side of the desk instead.

He patted his lapel. "I've just received confirmation from the earl. His lordship accepts your counteroffer."

He was actually patting his letter from Salt&Sea, not a missive from the earl. His lordship's directive had been communicated before Patrick left London with an impossible-to-misconstrue *Bring me that deed or you'll get the sack.*

Stanley beamed in delight. "That's wonderful news. You cannot imagine what it is like for me as a father of three daughters. We have the necessities, but I've been unable to spoil them as is their due. Without an appropriate dowry, their marital prospects were dim indeed. But now! Neither I nor they need worry again."

Everything was going exactly to plan. Patrick had brokered the agreement he'd set out to achieve. This was the precise moment to slide a pen and a provisional contract across the desk, and follow the signatures with a healthy toast of the offered brandy.

The earl would be pleased. The improved wages were imminent, as were Patrick's shares in the new venture's profits. Stanley Cartwright was thrilled with the new development. The forthcoming windfall was a boon to the man's entire family.

Almost the entire family.

Everybody won…except Deborah.

"What about the inn's current proprietress?" he asked as casually as he could.

"My sister-in-law?" Stanley let out a bark of laughter. "She certainly cannot work for a gaming hell. Can you imagine the scandal? I hope your earl wasn't depending on that."

"No, I mean… What will she do without the inn?"

Stanley stared at him blankly. "Do?"

"I heard she was once a professional soprano. Do you think she might sing again, once she's no longer encumbered by—"

"Perform on *stage?*" Stanley recoiled in obvious horror. "Good God, I think she knows better than that. Bad enough the folly of her youth is common knowledge. I certainly cannot have her soiling her reputation right when my girls finally have an opportunity to marry well."

Patrick clenched his jaw. He wanted to argue that singing was not sordid, and that stage performers were not synonymous with prostitution. But the fact was, a fair percentage of female acts *did* need to supplement their incomes by whatever means necessary. Patrick's views on the matter did not signify. Nor did Deborah's actual comportment, or the reasons wherefore.

Public perception was everything. As a father, Stanley would not wish his daughters' potential to be tainted by association.

As an aunt, the likelihood was that Deborah

would put her nieces' needs above her own. Leaving her with neither of her great passions. No opera and no inn. And possibly, no home.

"Has she…" He could not enquire about her finances. "…somewhere to go?" Ah, hell, he would just ask and be done with it. "Enough savings that she need not fear for her future?"

"Savings?" Stanley stared as though the thought was laughable. "Come the first of June, she won't even be able to afford the increase in rent necessary to justify a renewed contract."

"Does she know that? The first of June is only a fortnight away. She's been taking reservations as though she believes the inn will remain open without interruption for years to come."

"She's a romantic." Stanley shook his head as if bemused by such a characteristic. "That's why she dreamt up 'proof of purpose' as a determining factor."

"Proof of purpose?"

"She made me agree that if she could prove Siren's Retreat deserved to remain standing on merit alone, I would refrain from selling to a third party and renew her lease for another decade instead."

Patrick admired Deborah's ingenuity, creating a loophole out of pure determination. "Was she able to demonstrate particular merit?"

"She tried." Stanley slid open a drawer and tossed a large, leather-bound journal across the desk. "That's a copy of her reservation log. Every name of every guest since Siren's Retreat first opened its doors. She hoped the sheer volume of signatures would convince me not to sell, but no number of names is greater than the number my bank balance will see when the Earl of Edgewick transfers his payment."

Guilt suffused Patrick anew as he flipped through page after endless page of names. *His* employer's extravagant offer was the reason Deborah's impassioned pleas carried no weight. "May I keep this? Just for a few hours?"

Stanley shrugged. "It's of no use to me. Toss it in the rubbish when you're finished with it. Deborah has the original registry, not that it'll be any more than a souvenir soon enough. When does your employer plan on beginning new construction?"

The second of June, if Edgewick got his way. And the earl always got his way.

"Soon." Patrick tucked the book under his arm and rose to his feet. "I'll return on the first of June to sign the final contract, unless you change your mind before then."

"I won't," Stanley assured him. "Not now. At first, I was hesitant to sell. My brother built that inn with his bare hands. But with an offer like this!" Stanley made a *what-can-you-do* face. "Only a fool would choose sentimentality over money."

"Yes," Patrick muttered. "Only a fool."

He lurched from the study. He strode out of the

117

residence and sagged against a craggy wall around the corner and out of sight. Patrick rubbed his face. There had to be a way to resolve this matter without hurting Deborah. He hoped.

He had two weeks to find it.

Belatedly, he recalled the letter in his coat pocket from Salt&Sea. She was always a breath of fresh air. Perhaps her words would calm him now.

He opened the letter and read its contents, as charmed by the writer as he always was. He stopped halfway through and read a paragraph again. Apparently, someone Salt&Sea cared about was a liar who had betrayed her trust. The only person she still had faith in was LostInLondon, who had never lied to her. Unless one counted the mutual omission of names, in order to maintain their anonymity.

After her recent experience, Salt&Sea decided she was no longer willing to entertain any deceit in her relationships, including this epistolary one. LostInLondon was right. They should meet face-to-face. Tomorrow, at the Old Ship Inn's coffee room, just before sunset. It was the least popular hour for coffee, affording them relative privacy in a public venue. She would wear a yellow flower pinned to her bodice, so that he could recognize her.

She hoped their connection sparkled as much in life as it did in letters. Perhaps this was fate.

He folded the paper and groaned. He would meet her tomorrow, but he was going to be her second disappointment in as many days. Patrick treasured Salt&Sea's friendship, but he no longer wished to pursue her hand. His heart belonged to Deborah.

It was time to tell both women the truth.

.

CHAPTER 13

*P*atrick's heart beat faster as he approached the Old Ship Inn, a yellow flower in his hand.

He had ceased being romantically interested in Salt&Sea from the moment he met Deborah, but was very much looking forward to learning his correspondent's true name, and becoming friends in person. If their conversations were anything like their letters, he would not be surprised if hours passed in the blink of an eye.

Patrick stopped so suddenly in the doorway to the coffee room that he nearly tripped over his own feet.

Shite.

Deborah was here.

He was always happy to see her, of course. He'd spent the past night dreaming of her face, of her touch, of her kisses. He yearned to spend every night with her, and every day. Every hour.

But he hadn't planned on having her present to witness a rendezvous with another woman.

Deborah was skittish enough about giving love another chance. The last thing Patrick needed was to give her any reason to doubt the depth of his feelings.

He should approach her first. Explain why he was there. After all, his friendship with Salt&Sea was part of what had drawn him to Brighton, and to Deborah. Perhaps they even knew each other. Perhaps they would all become great friends, and this moment would become a favorite amusing anecdote to chuckle about as the years passed by.

Quickly, he glanced around the room. Empty. Salt&Sea wasn't here yet.

Patrick made his way toward Deborah. Her back was to him, her focus on the busy street outside the window. She seemed to sense his presence as he neared, and jerked her head over her shoulder with an expression of such joy, it was all he could do not to pull her into his arms and kiss her again as he had done beneath the elm trees.

The joy immediately vanished. Her face filled with loathing instead.

"Get out of here," she spat. "You'll ruin everything."

He blinked in confusion. The last time he'd seen her, they had been rolling on the grass in each other's arms, their mouths and bodies locked together.

"What's wrong? Are you vexed at…"

Then he saw it. The yellow flower. Pinned to her bodice.

Deborah was Salt&Sea.

"Vexed at you?" Her eyes flashed. "Yes, you could say I'm vexed at you. I would slap your face if you were worth the time. You pretended to be kind, pretended to be my friend, went so far as to… And all the while, you've been plotting to steal my home and destroy everything I've created and care for."

Salt&Sea's letter. Of course. *He* was the duplicitous villain who had betrayed her trust.

Betrayed Deborah.

The woman he had wanted all along, no matter what her name was.

He swung the hand with the yellow flower behind his back and crushed it inside his fist. This was not the time to disappoint her twice over. If he wanted any hope of forever, he first had to salvage this moment. Somehow.

"That isn't entirely true," he began.

She scoffed. "Which part do I have wrong? That you came here to purchase the land my inn resides on, and failed to mention that detail? Or the part where you intend to knock down my home and put a gaming hell in its place?"

He could not argue with either of these accusations.

"I wasn't pretending to be your friend," he said instead. "I was hoping we could become more than—"

"You must be deluded. I hope never to see you

again. You are despicable and a liar. How you can sleep at night—"

"I slept dreaming of you," he blurted. "As I've done since the moment we met. Which wasn't until *after* I arrived in Brighton. You can't expect me to have opposed my employer's wishes before I even met you—"

"You certainly made no attempt to do so after we did meet!" She sprang to her feet. "My lease has not yet expired, and already you've drafted contracts to buy my land out from under me without so much as a word of warning—"

"It's not your land," he enunciated. "It belongs to your brother-in-law. And your lease expires in six days. Did you expect him to do nothing to prepare, then flounder at the last minute to replace lost funds—"

"I didn't expect him to replace me at all!" She jabbed a finger in his cravat. "He would not have done, if *you* had not come along with your bags of bottomless gold. I dedicated my life to Siren's Retreat, and you want to turn it into—"

His voice rose to meet hers. "My wants do not enter the matter. I am not my employer. He sends me to acquire properties, and I acquire them. It's just business. If your emotions were not clouding your ability to reason—"

"Just business!" She leaned closer, until their lips were almost touching. "Was it your employer's business driving your actions beneath the elm trees? Or

ERICA RIDLEY

are you simply an unprincipled, self-serving, oppor-
tunistic—"

"You were there, too! I did not force you to place
your mouth—"

"I shan't do it again, that's for certain. Not with
you. I need you to leave at once, before you spoil my
chances with a man who is the absolute opposite of
you in every imaginable way. A gentleman who
knows the meaning of the word. A true friend, who
would never deceive another in the shameless
manner you find so simple to justify."

"I doubt you know him as well as you think you
do," he said bitterly, shoving the mutilated flower
petals deep into his pocket. "Every man is human
and fallible and not half the paragon you think he is,
because your fairy tales don't exist. Neither does the
angel you think you're waiting for."

"You don't know anything about me or him," she
spat. "He knows me better than anyone else alive,
and I him. A cad like you could never understand. I
do not need to explain myself. *You* certainly felt no
need to be forthcoming about yourself with me."

"Deborah—"

"You've already ruined enough. Leave now,
before you take the last thing I care about away
from me, too."

CHAPTER 14

*D*eborah flung her arm out and jabbed her finger toward the coffee room door. "Goodbye, Patrick."

At first, she thought he would argue. He stood unmoving, every muscle stiff. His jaw visibly clenched, his eyes surprisingly pained, as though it had never occurred to him that casually destroying people's homes and dreams likewise destroyed any hope of friendship or romance between them.

"Good day," he said tightly.

He marched from the coffee room without further argument, leaving Deborah alone with her thoughts amongst the empty tables.

Quickly, she checked the hour on the clock in the corner. Five minutes still remained before Lost-InLondon was to arrive. She smoothed her skirts and debated pinching her cheeks for color. She didn't want to appear pasty-faced and waxen because of her row with Patrick. She went ahead and pinched them.

It was a good thing she had come at the hour least likely to appeal to coffee drinkers. No one had overheard the heated conversation, which meant— she hoped—no one knew of Siren's Retreat's impending demise.

She could not quite wrap her mind about it. Was not even attempting it, to be honest. Six days remained in her lease, which meant there was still a chance, however slim, of convincing her brother-in-law not to go through with the sale.

Right?

She swung her gaze back to the clock rather than continue this line of thought. One minute until the hour. Approximately. These clocks were notoriously inexact. There could be five minutes left to wait...or LostInLondon could already be five minutes late.

Not that she would blame him. If he was lost in London, navigating unfamiliar Brighton would not be any easier. He might rush through the door full of pretty apologies, desperate to make a fine first impression. The moment could immortalize itself as The Moment They First Met, bringing fond smiles to their lips every time they reminisced about the day they met in the flesh.

Was the clock ticking louder? Had she even noticed it ticking before? Or was the coffee room so unsettlingly *empty* that she could not help but hear every tiny sound? The clock, her breaths, her heart, the rumble of carriages passing on the other side of the window.

He was distressingly late. Five minutes, ten minutes, did it matter? It would be an amusing story one day. It *would*. So long as he did eventually dash into the room in a cloud of—

Footsteps sounded in the corridor.

Deborah spun her head so quickly, she got a crick in her neck for her trouble.

Not LostInLondon. It was her friend Allegra Sharp, likely fresh from playing the pianoforte in her husband's tea shop. Deborah's shoulders slumped in disappointment for barely a second before she stiffened her spine and forced her face into a sunny smile.

Allegra slid into the seat opposite Deborah. "No sign of him yet?"

"He's not *very* late," Deborah said loyally. Fifteen minutes. Possibly twenty. Twenty-five. All right, he was very late. "Anything might have held him up. His valet… His horse throwing a shoe…"

"Pirate invasion… A bad batch of quail soup…"

"He'll be here. I *know* him. He's kind and sweet and thoughtful. He would never break a promise without at least sending a note." She held up a folded letter. "He confirmed again less than two hours ago."

Allegra tilted her head. "Why meet here, and not Siren's Retreat? You can't have been afraid to succumb to your own legend. Not if the two of you were halfway in love without ever meeting each other at all."

"I never said that," Deborah hedged.

Halfway in love. What a nonsense phrase. Halfway had seemed so far along, so close to a yes. And then Patrick had shown up and thrown everything into disarray. She shifted in her seat. For a moment, Patrick had made her think she was halfway in love with *him*. For a while now, if she were being honest. Long enough to feel guilty about what she would have to say to LostInLondon when they met.

And now, also thanks to Patrick, there was no need to mention him to LostInLondon at all. That bubble had popped like a balloon, their once-easy flirtation now impossible to put back together.

Patrick hadn't merely disappointed her. He'd deceived her. Whereas LostInLondon cared about every mundane moment in Deborah's life, Patrick hadn't given her feelings or her future the least consideration. Good riddance to him. She was definitely awaiting the better man.

Here, in a coffee room several streets away from Siren's Retreat.

Where there were no pesky legends about love at first sight to muddy the waters.

Allegra glanced at the clock. "Are you certain you agreed upon—"

"Yes. I do realize he's half an hour late. He'll be here."

Allegra nodded. "I believe you. I assume you put Nancy at the counter?"

"She's doing much better," Deborah gushed, relieved at the change in subject. "In a few weeks, I will feel perfectly comfortable leaving her in charge of the reception area for hours at a time…"

A few weeks. Would she even have that luxury? What if Stanley was so confident about selling the land out from under her, that he forbade his daughter from continuing to act as Deborah's assistant in the meantime? How could she chase new clients capable of paying higher rents if she could no longer step away from the counter?

Footsteps sounded in the corridor again. A *lot* of footsteps.

Half a dozen gentlemen strode into the room. None of them gave a second glance to Deborah and her wilting yellow flower. Now that the sun had set, the charms of the beach had lessened, and the coffee room would become more and more crowded.

She glanced at the clock again. Forty-five minutes late.

Possibly fifty. Or fifty-five.

Allegra lay a gentle hand against her shoulder. "Deborah…"

Acid churned in Deborah's stomach. The acid of disappointment. Of embarrassment. There was no need to pinch her cheeks now. She could feel her face flaming from the mortification of being jilted by a man she'd never even met.

"He's not coming, is he?" Her voice was hoarse.

Not even audible over the boisterous conversation of the gentlemen at the table next to them.

The sympathy in Allegra's face only made Deborah's mortification worse.

"Anything could have happened," Allegra offered, but Deborah no longer believed it.

LostInLondon had *chosen* not to come. He had let her sit here, rather than write a note to tell her he would not be coming. To admit that he didn't *want* to meet her.

Or, worse, maybe he'd glimpsed the widow with the drooping yellow flower through the window as he passed, and decided to keep on walking.

"That does it." She lifted her chin. "I'm done with men. And with love."

"You can't be done with love," Allegra pointed out. "What about Siren's Retreat?"

"It may be done with me," Deborah admitted. Her heart gave a pang of denial. "My lease expires at the end of the month, and the renewal price is more than I can afford. Stanley wants to sell the land. His buyer plans to turn Siren's Retreat into a gaming hell."

Allegra gasped in horror. "We can't let him!"

"Have you got an extra thousand pounds lying about?"

Allegra winced. "We haven't an extra penny. Everything went into the new tea room. It's doing phenomenally, and by this time next year—"

"I don't have until next year." Deborah stared down at the table. "I have until Monday."

"What will you do?"

Deborah rose to her feet and straightened her spine. "Fight any way that I can."

Allegra smiled. "I'll help."

CHAPTER 15

*P*atrick let himself into the rooms he was renting, nausea churning in his gut.

He'd been the luckiest man in the world twice over: Salt&Sea was indeed everything he'd imagined her to be and more. Deborah Cartwright was the perfect woman for him in every way. They were the same person. Destiny had led him to her *twice*.

And he had mucked up his chance both times.

He yanked the window curtains closed. There was nothing to see outside but darkness. That's all there was inside of himself, too. He had left Deborah sitting there at an otherwise empty table, waiting in innocent hope for a man Patrick well knew would never appear.

Or rather, he'd been standing right in front of her. Proving himself unworthy with every breath. She had ordered him from her sight. Who could blame her?

He *was* in Brighton to purchase the land beneath her feet. He *hadn't* confessed his full agenda.

Both facts were conditions of his continued employment. Not that *It's my job* was much of an argument. Cold comfort to the woman who would soon lose *her* post, if Patrick performed his correctly.

Just like he would lose his post if he let her keep hers.

Patrick slumped into the chair before the writing desk, propped his elbows on its smooth mahogany surface, and dropped his face into his hands.

He hadn't meant to hurt her. But both sides of himself had let Deborah down. Personal and professional. He'd botched his chance to apologize as himself, and now he owed her one as LostInLondon as well.

Lost. That's how he felt, all right. A disorienting sensation after knowing exactly what to do for all his life. His decisiveness, efficiency, and quick, cold logic were the traits that made him such an exemplary man of business.

They were also what had made him lose Deborah.

He lifted his face from his hands. Was that true? Had he ever *had* her? Or had she always been a fantasy, forever out of reach? She was everything he'd dreamt she'd be, and he was nothing but a nightmare come true for her. She would never forgive him. Not Patrick the man, nor LostIn-

London from their earnest, anonymous correspondence.

Letters. That was the one thing he was good at,
was it not? Or had been. There was nothing he
could tell Deborah that she wanted to hear. Neither
he nor his epistolary alternate were the man she
hoped he would be.

But there must be something he could do.

Patrick sifted through the piles on his desk until
he came to the journal Stanley Cartwright had
given him. A copy of the guest registry for Siren's
Retreat, dating back to the morning the doors first
opened for business.

He paged through it absently. Most of the names
he did not recognize, but several, he did. Members
of the aristocracy, business acquaintances of the
Earl of Edgewick. Some of which had likely had
more correspondence with Patrick than with the
earl himself.

Quickly, he pulled a sheaf of blank parchment
closer and uncapped his bottle of ink. A proper man
of business made no move without investigating all
angles. He would send inquiries to every name in
this book, if need be. Perhaps someone, somewhere,
would say the one thing that would spark an idea
on how to unmuck this muddle.

Patrick's fingers ached. The stack of outgoing
correspondence had grown exponentially by the
time he realized what he was really doing: procras-
tinating the letter he *ought* to be writing.

Apologizing to the person who deserved more than he could ever give.

Guilt clawed from inside his ribs. He closed the journal and pushed the pile of unsent letters away. It was time to write the only one that mattered.

My darling Salt&Sea,

NO, absolutely not. Deborah would not be in a "darling" frame of mind, after needlessly waiting for a suitor who never bothered to appear.

His chest clenched. How long *had* she waited? Surely not long after Patrick left. Right? He remembered how she looked in front of the large mullioned windows, the soft colors of sunset reflecting prettily on her hopeful face.

The sky would have gone darker and darker. The night colder and colder. The chair in front of her ever more empty. Her stomach ever more certain that the man she was waiting for was never going to show.

No. Patrick had lost all rights to "darling". He crumpled the page and began anew.

Dear Salt&Sea,

ERICA RIDLEY

NOT THAT, either. It was classic, generic, ordinary…
and yet somehow still felt presumptuous. She
wasn't his dear just like she wasn't his darling. If he
started like this, she wouldn't even read to the
second word. The letter would go straight into the
closest fire.

My fervent apologies.

THERE. Get the most important part out of the
way first. If she read nothing more, at least she
would have glimpsed the heart of the matter. He
did not expect her to forgive him, but at least she
would know that the slight had not been done
glibly.

He kept writing:

*There was nothing I wanted more than to meet you in
person. I have longed for this moment for months.
Nothing would have kept me from keeping our date.*

EXCEPT SOMETHING OBVIOUSLY HAD, from her point
of view. He paused as he debated what to say and
how to say it. The truth was, this was not the sort of
apology one could weasel out of, via words on

136

paper. This was an apology that needed to happen face-to-face.

If she would let him.

You are owed a complete and honest explanation. I hope that you will give me the opportunity to provide you with a full accounting, after which I will abide by whatever decision you make, with regard to our

WITH THEIR WHAT? Friendship? Courtship? Flirtation? It was Patrick who had held her in his arms, Patrick who had kissed her. Not Lost-InLondon.

with regard to continuing our acquaintance. Please give me one more chance. I will meet you at the same time, at the same place, on the evening of

WHEN? Tomorrow? She was owed the most expedient apology possible, and yet Patrick hesitated to promise it to her.

The truth was...he didn't want her to forgive LostInLondon. That was a pseudonym, an illusion. He wanted her to forgive Patrick Gretham the man, not an anonymous letter-writer.

He wanted her to see *him* as viable.

But he knew that if he confessed his dual identity at this point, she would reject him out of hand and he would lose her forever. He needed to prove to her that she and her mortal enemy *Patrick* were indeed a perfect match. Only then might she be able to reconcile her feelings toward both men, once she knew them to be one and the same—and that she held his heart in her hands.

But he was running out of time.

31 May.

THE NIGHT before her lease expired. By then, Patrick would have found a solution…or not. And Deborah would forgive him…or not.

He would reveal all aspects of himself by that date, come what may. He had six days to change her mind and convince her to give him another chance.

The clock was ticking.

CHAPTER 16

While Nancy presided over the reception area, Deborah and Allegra bent their heads together over one of the three small tables in front of the counter. Usually, Deborah placed the morning newspapers atop each square table for her guests' convenience.

Today, she and Allegra were using the middle table to plot out stratagems.

"Multi-year commitments," Allegra suggested. "All reservations must be for at least three seasons, paid in full up front."

Deborah shook her head. "We'll have fewer reservations. And while it would generate more money in the short term, it wouldn't increase income overall."

"We're not worried about 'overall' yet," Allegra pointed out. "What you need at this moment is enough coin in your pocket to convince your brother-in-law to sign another lease."

Deborah dutifully wrote it down.

"What about a lending library?" Nancy called out. "Those are profitable."

Allegra rubbed her chin. "Brighton has several lending libraries already. And there's the small detail of needing to stock the library with purchases in order to have inventory to rent out."

"What if I didn't buy the inventory?" Deborah mused aloud. "What if I offered…toys from the local toymaker? The guests' children would love the novelty and beg to keep their favorite items. We could send a stream of business straight to the toymaker for a small commission on each sale."

"That's good," Allegra said, impressed. "Write that down."

Deborah's pen scratched over the paper. "We need something bigger."

"Something that will turn a profit faster than a commission on dolls."

"Something they can only get here. The toymaker's shop is on the main square, and there are a dozen other inns. It has to be something exclusively available here."

"You have that. Everyone knows the legend of Siren's Retreat. One need only cross your threshold with an open heart to find one's destiny." Allegra touched her chest and grinned. "I'm living proof that it works."

"Embroidered handkerchiefs!" Nancy called out. "Each one with 'I found my true love at Siren's Retreat' written around the edges. We can create another set for those on honeymoon, or celebrating their wedding anniversary."

Deborah wrote it down, despite her misgivings. "Embroidery is time-consuming, and no more profitable than a commission on dolls. It needs to be something tourists would be willing to pay a fortune for. Something they'd come for miles to have."

Allegra nodded, deep in thought. "Something they could boast to their friends about."

"Well," Nancy said. "That's simple enough. You're already doing it."

Deborah frowned. "I'm already doing what?"

"Not you. I meant Allegra. Tourists turn their holiday schedules upside-down and purchase more tea than they could ever drink, in the hopes of being present at Sharp's Tea Room when Allegra pops in to play the pianoforte."

"How does her music help Siren's Retreat?"

"Not hers. *Yours.*" Nancy leaned her elbows onto the counter. "You're a famous opera singer—"

"Not famous anymore," Deborah demurred. "I haven't seen a stage this decade."

"And yet, people still know your name. You're the reason they visited Siren's Retreat in the beginning, before there *was* a legend. All the tourists who have ever seen you perform brag about it to those who have not."

"You're suggesting I...sing for my supper?" Deborah said doubtfully. "Climb onto the counter at random intervals to perform an aria or two?"

"Private singing *lessons*," Nancy said with satisfaction. "From the top soprano in all of England herself. At an exorbitant fee, and exclusively available to paying guests. A lesson with you would be like sharing a sliver of your fame. You're the siren of Siren's Retreat. Who wouldn't pay for the chance to be a siren for the day, too?"

Deborah stared at her niece in wonder. It was a wonderful idea. It could work. It *would* work.

"Write that down," Allegra whispered.

Deborah pushed the list away. "I don't have to. That's it. I already have a parlor with a small pianoforte. My instrument is nothing like yours, of course—"

"But I'd still be happy to play it for you." Allegra grinned at her.

Deborah's chest lightened with hope for the first time in weeks. "You'd be my accompanist?"

"It would be my honor." Allegra winked. "As would my commission."

"Both of you at once?" Nancy squealed. "The price just tripled!"

Deborah laughed and pulled out a fresh sheet of parchment. "I shall design the announcement at once. I can leave a few advertisements interspersed strategically with the daily newspapers, post dozens about town, leave stacks for the taking at the milliner's and the—"

The door to the inn swung open and the postman stepped inside.

Ever since she'd first began corresponding with

LostInLondon, the mere sight of the postman caused Deborah's heart to jump and her blood to rush faster.

Today, however, she was merely irritated at the interruption. Who cared what the inconsiderate clod who had jilted her last night was up to? She was going to save Siren's Retreat!

Even when the postman handed over the letter and Deborah recognized the handwriting on top, her chest simply felt empty. If LostInLondon didn't respect her time, he wasn't worth her heart.

"Is that from…" Allegra bounced her eyebrows in the direction of the letter.

"Yes." Deborah tossed it aside.

"Aren't you going to read it?"

"I don't care what he has to say."

"Can *I* read it?"

Deborah sighed and broke the seal. She scanned the letter's contents in silence.

Allegra leaned forward. "Has he a good excuse for his absence?"

"He says he does." Deborah read the letter again. "Actually, he very carefully *doesn't* claim that he has a *good* excuse. Just that there *is* a reason, which he wishes to explain to me at the same time, at the same place, on the last day of the month."

Allegra groaned. "Five days from now? It feels like forever. Why the wait?"

Deborah handed her the letter. "He doesn't say."

"He does say he's sorry, and sounds like he

means it." Allegra looked up from the letter. "Are you going to go?"

"I suppose he'll find out on the thirty-first," Deborah joked lightly. But the tell-tale butterflies were back in her stomach.

Should she go? Should she trust him? What if he failed to show again? She would be twice the fool, with only herself to blame for believing they shared something special, when they did not.

On the other hand, what if they were meant to be? This could be her last opportunity to find out.

She plucked the letter from Allegra's hands and tucked it beneath the list of ideas to save her inn.

"Where were we? Ah, yes. How much should we charge for each lesson?"

DEBORAH WAS ALONE behind the counter later that afternoon, refining the design of the bill she planned to reproduce and post all over town, when the front door to the inn opened and a man stepped inside. Not the harried postman this time with yet another letter.

Patrick Gretham, in the flesh.

Deborah slid the handbill she was working on out of sight. "I've said all I intend to say—"

"Then please listen, just for a moment." His hand emerged from behind his back, bearing a bright bouquet of spring flowers. "I'm sorry. I am sorry I disappointed you, and I am sorry I deceived you.

That I was instructed to keep mum about my business until it was complete does not mitigate the pain I caused you."

"That's...true." Deborah crossed her arms. It was a good apology. But him being sorry that he was here to destroy life as she knew it did not change the fact that he was here to do exactly that.

He stepped closer and held out the flowers.

Deborah did not want to take them. That was partly why she had kept her arms firmly crossed. Taking his flowers felt like accepting his apology, and accepting the apology felt like accepting the man, and accepting the man felt like accepting his plans to demolish her romantic retreat, and that was the one thing she could never accept.

Patrick's handsome face lost some of its hopefulness, but his hand did not waver. He seemed prepared to stand in her reception area all day, arm outstretched, a bouquet springing forth from his fist like a god of abundance bestowing a gift of agricultural delights.

Then again, in the myths, wasn't it Hades who held the cornucopia? Fitting, given Patrick's intent to turn her heaven-on-earth into a gaming hell.

"I *am* sorry." Arm still outstretched, he dropped to his knees. "I beg you to believe me when I say—"

"*Stand up*," she whispered, darting an appalled glance toward the front window. If her nosy neighbors were to walk by and spy him on bended knee, they would assume Patrick was in the midst of—

A silver-brown curl of hair tumbled over his

brow as he rose back to his feet, making him look all the more roguish and charming than usual. Belatedly, she realized that the bouquet in his hand wasn't simply spring flowers, but her *favorite* flowers. White primrose and yellow daffodils and a plethora of sweet violets. A detail she had never once shared with him. The blackguard clearly had the devil's own luck.

"It's an olive branch," he coaxed. "I will find you a literal one, if it would make a difference."

Humph. He probably would.

Grudgingly, she unfolded her arms from her chest and accepted the beautiful bouquet. "This doesn't mean I forgive you for wanting to knock down my home and replace it with a horrid gambling den."

"I understand that I'm the enemy. But I don't want to be. If it were in my power to do anything else—"

"Isn't it? Can't you just…refuse?" Deborah knew even as she said the words how naïve they sounded.

"If I balk, my employer will simply find someone else who *will* follow orders. Likely that same day. I am a cog, not the machine."

Deborah stared down at the flowers. She knew what he was saying was true. He had not come here with the intent to ruin her life and everything she had worked toward. One could argue they were both doing their jobs as best they could, in the circumstances they'd been given. He wasn't a bad person. He was a soldier for the opposite side.

And this was war.

"I won't let you take Siren's Retreat from me," she said firmly.

"I don't want to take it from you," he promised.

His hazel eyes showed pain, not malice. He didn't want to hurt her. She believed him, damn it. He had no wish to do this terrible thing.

But he would.

CHAPTER 17

*W*hen Patrick brought more daffodils, primrose, and violets the following afternoon, Deborah arched her brows.

"Are you going to bring flowers every day?"

"Until it works or I leave Brighton," he answered matter-of-factly. "Whichever comes first."

The thought of him leaving, never to return, did not fill her with as much satisfaction and relief as she might have expected. Instead, her belly hollowed as though her body already missed him. Not that he needed to know such things. He already had the upper hand in their current negotiations. She would not add "yearning for their doomed romance" to the list.

"Until the flowers succeed with what?" she asked instead.

"Convincing you that I am in earnest." His eyes were serious, his voice soft. "I value having you in my life. I am sorrier than you can know."

"One way or the other, I won't be in your life for long. If you turn my inn into a gambling den, I won't step foot on these grounds again. And if I convince Stanley that Siren's Retreat is worth more than its current value on the market, and that renewing my lease is the wisest business decision he'll make all year, even your wealthy employer won't be able to—"

"Is that what you're trying to do?" Patrick's face lit with interest. "What are your arguments?"

"As if I'd tell you." But her eyes betrayed her by darting toward the freshly printed handbills stacked under the registration ledger.

He moved the book out of the way and lifted the topmost advertisement. "Singing lessons! It's brilliant. And with Mrs. Sharp as accompanist. Why waste five pence on tea in the hopes of catching a song or two, when you could spend five pounds to hear the two of you together for half an hour?"

Exactly the extravagant logic she was counting on her wealthier guests to espouse. Deborah was even planning on performing regular duets with Allegra at Sharp's Tea Room to help spread the word.

She held out her palm for the handbill. "Give the advert back."

"May I keep it?"

Before she could answer, loud footsteps and a rumble of voices sounded on the stairs, followed immediately by the appearance of a family renting one of the larger upstairs apartments. They all began asking Deborah questions at once, talking over each other to be heard.

"How does one reserve a bathing machine?"

"How do they work? Are there time limits? How do I get back inside after I've splashed down?"

"Where is the best place to play cards? Preferably whist. Not deep play, mind. Something friendly."

"With good wine and thick beefsteaks. Is there a place with cards and good beefsteak?"

"Which way to the tea room? Have you a map of the town?"

"Or a calendar of events? Which assembly room will host the next ball? Must we purchase a subscription if we're only here for the week?"

Deborah abandoned her conversation with Patrick in order to attend to her guests as best she could. She expected him to slip out quietly in the confusion. Instead, he let her deal with the dancing schedule and the town map, whilst he gave remarkably thorough answers on the vagaries of bathing machine operators, and which card rooms were best known for what play and good food.

She stumbled over her own words a time or two from listening too hard to his eloquent explanations. This was more than superficial trivia gleaned from guidebooks. He sounded like a local, not a tourist. His description of the Castle Inn's beefsteaks made her want to lock up shop and sit down for a meal posthaste. He sounded like he cared about Brighton. Like he cared about maintaining Siren's Retreat's reputation.

Like he cared about *her*.

When he met her stare, his gaze warmed. The corners of his eyes crinkled as if her mere proximity brought him pleasure and contentment, even if they were engaged in opposite tasks. They were a marvelous team.

He *did* care, damn him. His regard for her was plain to see, flowers or no flowers. Deborah cursed him beneath her breath.

Try as she might to resist him, her heart fluttered in his presence and sank in his absence. Despite hating what he came here to do, she could not hate the man. She cared about him just as much as she'd ever cared about LostInLondon—whom she hadn't thought about in an embarrassingly long time.

Her correspondent hadn't crossed her mind since the moment Patrick had first shown up with daffodils and primrose. She'd forgotten the jilting entirely...as well as LostInLondon's promise to meet in truth on the thirty-first of May, three days from now.

Once upon a time, there was nothing she would have awaited more eagerly. She'd thought LostInLondon was everything she could ever want. A second chance for companionship, for happiness, for love.

Today, the only thing Deborah was certain of was that the answers were never so easy.

IN TWO DAYS, Stanley would decide whether or not to renew Deborah's lease.

He had been unmoved by the copy of the guest registry containing all the names of all the happy customers over the years. Deborah hoped the increase in price for the finest apartments and the added revenue from the children's lending library and the exclusive voice lessons for adults would be enough to sway him.

She didn't have that money *yet*, but the response had been swift and enthusiastic. Word was spreading, and dozens of future guests had already written to add an hour or two of private instruction to their existing reservations.

If she would be forced to write back to all of those eager clients, informing them that not only would there be no lending library and no voice lessons, but there was also actually no reservation, because there would no longer be an inn to visit…

No, she would not allow such negative thoughts to permeate her mind. Siren's Retreat matched fated pairs on a regular basis, which meant this inn was *also* meant to be. Deborah would find a way, and destiny would handle the rest.

She hoped.

In the meantime, she had become disconcertingly accustomed to Patrick working by her side. He spent more hours behind the counter than Nancy—and was twice as talented, using his affable charm and gift of persuasion to drive up prices and coax wavering tourists to book their next holiday with Siren's Retreat.

Patrick materialized every morning in time to bring in the day's papers, and did not leave until nightfall, except to pop out around noon to bring back a hot meal from one of the local restaurants.

Deborah had told him this was unnecessary, that there was a perfectly capable kitchen here at Siren's Retreat. Patrick pointed out that Deborah rarely took advantage of her own kitchen, rarely pausing long enough to take a breath, much less a respite—and that Nancy was copying her every move.

Patrick did not intend to infringe on Deborah's hospitality, and if he was already fetching food for himself, why not bring back enough to share with both women, too?

What could Deborah say to that, except, *Thank you, that sounds lovely*? It was exactly how he turned idle passers-by into future guests. He just smiled his crooked smile, twinkled his hazel eyes, and spoke as if his suggestions were the most natural, foregone conclusions in the world.

If she'd had *him* as her assistant this past year, she and Stanley could carpet the floor in banknotes.

Not that Patrick was her assistant. Despite giving every impression that he wanted Siren's Retreat to survive, she knew very well which side his bread was buttered on. Lord knew, *she* was not paying him for the long hours he put in at her side. That was, unless one counted the richness of her kisses and the—

"Sunset." He put down the broom he'd been sweeping with and met Deborah's eyes. "Walk me to my inn?"

Her cheeks flushed and she avoided Nancy's shrewd gaze. "I'll get my bonnet."

Walking Patrick to his inn had begun as a jest. For one, his inn was literally across the street. He would not let her return alone, and insisted on accompanying her as a gentleman, thereby necessitating he walk to his own inn not once, but twice.

He said it gave him a chance to spend a few tranquil moments with Deborah away from the hustle and bustle of the reception area.

The stolen moments weren't particularly tranquil, now that they'd incorporated taking a meandering "short" cut through the elm groves where they'd shared their first kiss... And the second... And the third...

Soon, they were racing toward the trees like adolescents, tripping over the grass and each other as they sprinted arm-in-arm toward the cloaking cover of the elm grove.

He swung her over an exposed root and into his arms, wasting no time in covering her mouth with his for an unrestrained kiss.

She wrapped her arms about his neck and held on tight. He made her forget all the reasons why not. He had somehow become a part of her routine now. A part of her heart, which was beating wildly against his chest as it did every time he took her into his arms.

Foolish, she reminded herself. In two days' time, either she would win and he would go home, or he would have won, and she'd find herself without a home—and no interest in exchanging kisses with the man who took it from her. At that point, she wouldn't even be interested in exchanging *letters*.

Her heart thumped as the memory of a past letter bubbled to the surface.

She was supposed to meet LostInLondon tomorrow.

If her friend *did* possess a logical and unavoidable explanation for failing to appear at their last meeting, it would be churlish to deny him the opportunity to put things to rights. That was not the part that unnerved her.

What if the spark she'd once imagined she and LostInLondon would share...really was the fireworks she'd once hoped it would be? What if they got on even better than she and Patrick—a circumstance made all the more likely because sweet, gentle LostInLondon was not trying to buy her land out from under her. What if she *did* like him just as much, or better?

Then what was she doing here, with Patrick?

CHAPTER 18

*J*oy and hope pulsed through Patrick's blood as he kissed Deborah. These past days had been his last and only chance to prove himself worthy as a suitor as Patrick Gretham before Deborah discovered he was also LostInLondon. They were to meet in the coffee room tomorrow.

Slivers of doubt punctured his exuberance. Should he come clean now? Would she believe him, out of context? He wasn't carrying any old letters. Even if she did believe him, would she be happy? Or would the reveal be one more prolonged deception, yet more proof that he was not and had never been good enough?

LostInLondon was perfect, but Patrick was... Patrick. He could not extricate himself from his long and successful career as a man of business any more than Deborah could separate herself from Siren's Retreat.

Not that she had to. Patrick was here to shatter that bond for her.

As if reading his mind, Deborah tore her mouth from his and pushed away. "I can't do this."

He wanted to argue. To coax, to cajole, to negotiate. To hear an addendum of not doing this *at the current moment*, leaving open the glorious possibility of more kisses in the future. More anything. More everything.

He kissed her hands and pressed them to his pounding chest. If she could feel what was in his heart, would that make a difference?

And if the layers of his clothes were too thick, if he alone knew just how passionately his heart beat for her every moment of every day, then there was nothing else to do but drop to his knees and try to make her understand in words.

He dropped to the grass before her. The sun had almost set. In the shadows of the elm trees, her face was barely visible. He did not need the sun. Not when he had her. She was brighter, warmer, a thousand times more beautiful. He had every angle of her face memorized, every eyelash. The exact shade of her brilliant blue eyes and rose-petal-soft lips.

It was time to declare himself. Fate would take care of the rest.

"When I set out for Brighton, I did not know what treasure awaited. You are not only better than I imagined, I could not have dreamt how deeply and irrevocably I would fall for—"

"Patrick—"

157

"You are all that I want in this world. I am neither vain nor foolish enough to think you feel the same about me, but I am willing to spend the rest of my lifetime trying to change your mind. I am yours. Happily, wholeheartedly. Let me make you mine. I shall—"

"Patrick. I already know what you will do: Destroy us."

She tugged her hands from his and he knew that he had lost.

"Whether you go, or whether you stay, our futures divide us beyond repair."

"Deborah—"

She scrambled up from the grass. "Don't come back tomorrow. I'm busy. And tomorrow evening, I've an appointment with Stanley, at which time he will either renew my lease or he won't. If he does, you go. If he doesn't, I go. Either way…this is goodbye."

PATRICK TRUDGED TOWARD HIS LODGINGS. When he stepped through the front door, the proprietor pounced as though he'd been lying in wait for just this moment.

"There you are!"

Patrick removed his hat and ran a hand over his hair. "Were you looking for me?"

"Don't normally have to. You usually pop down a dozen times a day, gadding to or from the post office, and inquiring after correspondence here as though you fancy yourself the most fashionable man in England."

"Not the most fashionable," Patrick said. "Just an avid correspondent."

"Well, I see that now, don't I? You up and disappear all of a sudden—"

Patrick quickly did the calculation. He and Salt&Sea had exchanged no further communication after agreeing to meet. Not wanting to miss a word from her had been the driving force propelling him to check for correspondence so many times a day. But for the past several days, there'd been no need to. He'd been by her side from dawn to dusk, she and her words never more than an arm's reach away.

He missed her already. He no doubt always would.

"—and now I've got more letters than kindling," the proprietor continued. "If you don't take this stack soon, that's exactly what I'll do with it. Let the kitchen staff feed it to the oven to bake our bread. Lord knows, it would take me the rest of my life just to *read* all of this—"

"What? Letters? For me?"

"Letters? For you? Ha!" The proprietor hefted a large canvas sack off the floor and shoved it into Patrick's arms. "My counter is not your private desk, sir. I shall have no choice but to enact a surcharge if you continue to presume—"

"I'll pay double your rate for the rest of my stay to thank you for your kindness."

"Oh. Well, then. That's all right. Carry on with you. You'll be up all night just figuring out what's what in all that mess. I'll have one of the maids send up an extra candle."

Patrick climbed the stairs with the sack of letters and dumped them atop a chaise longue rather than his small writing desk in order to have more space. For a brief second, he was bewildered by the sight of his name written in so many unfamiliar hands.

Then he remembered the inquiries he had sent out to the addresses listed in the Siren's Retreat guest log.

Quickly, he sorted the letters into piles based on names anyone would recognize—Lord This, Lady That—and those he did not. Once the stacks were organized to his liking, he began with the letters from ordinary people.

After the first five or six, it was clear they could have all been written by the same hand:

Marvelous... magical... life-changing... luckiest man in the world... luckiest woman in the world... found the love of my life... never been happier... fate... destiny... forever indebted... owe it all to Siren's Retreat...

HE OPENED the responses from the aristocracy to more of the same. Blissfully happy couple after blissfully happy couple, each without fail crediting Siren's Retreat as the source of their joy and good fortune, extolling it as the superlative, unskippable destination for honeymoons and celebrating all subsequent anniversaries.

Patrick rubbed his face. Stanley Cartwright might not see what he had, but Patrick had no such difficulty. How could Patrick possibly turn this historic, beloved landmark into a smoky, sordid gambling hell?

Unfortunately, the other side to that question was: how could he not?

If Patrick refused to complete his assigned tasks as instructed, the earl would simply dismiss him and hire a new man of business who would do the job. Likely even the same day. And then what would Patrick's grand gesture have been worth? Exactly nothing.

Either way, the walls of Siren's Retreat were coming down.

Patrick pushed up from the chaise longue and crossed over to his desk. The paper lying on top was the handbill he'd been unable to stop staring at all week.

Deborah's advertisement for music lessons.

She had such a magnificent voice and extraordinary talent, and was so enthusiastic about sharing her love of music and singing with future guests. This handbill wasn't only a desperate attempt to hold on to her inn and home. It was a symbol of her hopes and dreams, her optimism, her confidence. Her belief that all paths led to destiny, and that Siren's Retreat was her fate, her fortune, and her future.

Patrick stared down at the handbill. He could not, would not, give up on Siren's Retreat—or on Deborah. Which meant, ineffective as the gesture might be, he could not be the villain who tore down her dreams and took away her home. Even if it meant walking away from his comfortable, ascendant post and losing his own fortune.

He glanced at the clock on the mantel. If he left now, he could be back in London by midnight, meet with the earl in the morning, be packed up and gone before noon, and be back to Brighton just in time for sunset...and his meeting with Salt&Sea.

Of course, any number of things could go wrong with that plan. The earl might spend the night at his clubs and not rise until two or three in the afternoon, making a return to Brighton before nightfall impossible. Or everything could go to plan, only for an axle to break, or a horse to twist an ankle in a pothole, or the rain to wash out a road right when Patrick needed it most.

No. He could not risk failing to keep his promise to Salt&Sea. To Deborah. He intended to be there early this time. To spend all day in that coffee room if necessary.

Which meant he could not possibly pay a call on

the Earl of Edgewick. A man in love had priorities. Deborah came first, now and forever.

Especially if tomorrow was Patrick's last chance to tell her.

He sat at his desk and pushed the handbill aside. He would write a letter, that's what he would do. Patrick had been sending daily briefs to the earl during the entire trip. He would write an even more eloquent letter here and now.

His pen flew across the page.

The fact of the matter was that Siren's Retreat should remain Siren's Retreat. It was Patrick's opinion as the earl's man of business, and also as a human being with eyes and a soul and a heart. Despite his lordship's statements to the contrary, not everything in life was about profit and personal glory. Siren's Retreat was a destination, a symbol, a home, a new beginning.

Siren's Retreat was love.

Siren's Retreat was hope.

Siren's Retreat was destiny.

Although Patrick would always hold the earl in great esteem, honor dictated he could not continue working for someone who valued only that which brought him money.

His lordship should therefore consider this letter Patrick's official resignation.

When he finished, he reread his words three times, then four, adding new bits and striking out others until it was a polished pearl of persuasion. Or at least, the best a desperate man could do at the eleventh hour. He carefully rewrote each paragraph onto new parchment one final time, then set the pages aside to dry.

The letter would be sealed and in the hands of a competent courier within a quarter hour. There was nothing else to do tonight.

Tomorrow, Patrick would meet Deborah as himself—the best self he was capable of being. If she still rejected him, at least he would have tried everything in his power to ensure she could keep the life she deserved.

With or without Patrick in it.

CHAPTER 19

*T*he sun would not set for another hour and a half, but Deborah was already in her dressing chamber, tidying her hair. The extra effort was not *strictly* for LostInLondon. Her meeting with her brother-in-law was right before the scheduled time in the coffee room.

But she was not primping for Stanley. Whatever path he intended to take, the decision was already reached. Deborah's artfully curled tendrils and favorite emerald dress would not hold any partic-ular sway.

It was LostInLondon in whose honor she had spent the past hour bathing and perfuming and ironing and curling.

Deborah hoped she was not being foolish.

Again.

LostInLondon had already failed to put in an appearance once. If he did not bother to turn up as promised tonight…

She would still have Patrick, whispered a shadowy corner of her mind.

Except she didn't have Patrick, did she? Deborah had told him not to return, and he had respected her wishes. She had not set eyes on him since leaving him speechless at the elm grove the night before.

Part of her had thought he would disregard her feelings and appear just after dawn with the morning newspapers as he'd done all week. Part of her had waited for him all day, thrumming with anticipation, jumping every time the door opened. Pretending nonchalance in case it was him this time.

It never was. It never would be again.

Deborah accidentally met her own eyes in the looking-glass, and her gaze slid away. Now that goodbye was final, she could not help but wish their last conversation had ended differently.

To be more precise, she wished she and Patrick had not ended at all.

The truth was, LostInLondon was perfect on paper, but Deborah had fallen in love with imperfect, flesh-and-blood Patrick instead. He was sweet and charming and driven and infuriating and worked for the devil himself, as far as Deborah was concerned. That was, when Patrick wasn't working for *her*, free of charge, driving up prices and taking down reservations as though cared just as much about Siren's Retreat as he did about…

Her.

She strode from her dressing chamber on wobbly knees, and did not manage to leave her thoughts behind. She had interrupted Patrick's declaration of love precisely *because* that was the direction she had suspected he was heading. When in fact what she could have done, what she *should* have done, was follow his declaration with her own.

He was not easy. Their path was anything but simple. But she did not want to take another step if it wasn't in tandem. She'd loved having him literally by her side every day. She loved *him*. There was no use denying it.

After meeting with Stanley and LostInLondon, she would find Patrick and tell him so.

Love was forever—and much bigger than any two hearts could hold. Lightning *did* strike twice. Fate always found a way. She didn't know what it was yet, but they could weather that storm together.

If Patrick was still here in Brighton, that was. Deborah had told him not to come back. What if he'd obeyed her command to the letter, and had already returned to London?

Worse, what if destiny had other plans for him altogether?

WHEN DEBORAH ARRIVED at her brother-in-law's residence, his butler Fenton could best be described as being in a tizzy.

"Oh!" Fenton stared at Deborah as if he'd never

seen her before and was not at all certain what to do with her now that she was here. Usually, he waved her in with smile and no questions asked, but today he hovered in the middle of the doorway, vibrating like a tuning fork.

"Is Stanley in his study?" Deborah prompted gently.

"Oh," Fenton said again. "Well, yes. He's here. And in his study. But I'm not certain he's receiving, and should not at all like to interrupt him while he's entertaining."

Entertaining? *Stanley?*

"He's expecting me," Deborah assured the butler as she squeezed past him.

Entertaining who, when he had a scheduled appointment with Deborah? Perhaps that was the answer. Perhaps *she* was the answer. Perhaps he had champagne on ice to celebrate the renewal of her lease.

"Er…that may be," stammered Fenton. "But I really don't think this is the time—"

Deborah was already down the corridor, rushing into Stanley's study out of breath and eager to put paid to the past months of interminable anxiety.

"What did you decide?" she blurted as she skidded into the room.

Stanley looked at her as if he, too, had forgotten she existed, and was not quite certain what to do with her, now that she'd materialized where she was least expected.

At the exact time and location of their planned meeting.

"Oh." He blinked at her. "Deborah."

"Stanley." She dipped a curtsey and fumbled for social niceties. "How do you do? It's a lovely evening, isn't it? Are you renewing my lease?"

It was then that she noticed they were not alone in the study. Standing in front of the brandy buffet on the opposite wall from Stanley's enormous desk was a tall man with white whiskers, a comfortable paunch to his belly, and clothing that looked as though it had cost more than she earned in a year. He looked as regal as a painting of a prince.

"Lord Edgewick, if you'll pardon the interruption." Stanley cleared his throat. "This is my sister-in-law, Mrs. Deborah Cartwright."

Lord Edgewick? Who the dickens was that?

For his part, Lord Edgewick stared at Deborah with equal parts confusion and curiosity, clearly just as befuddled to find a stranger in the midst as she was herself.

"An *earl*," Stanley mouthed.

She dipped another curtsey. A grand one this time. In part due to the earl's rank, but mostly out of embarrassment for having barged in like a wild pig without pausing to take note of her surroundings. As though displaying her prettiest manners now would somehow wipe the mental image of her graceless arrival from the earl's mind.

"His lordship's man of business resigned abruptly late last night," Stanley explained, as though this explanation meant anything at all to her.

She shifted her weight. "I'm...sorry to hear that?"

"Yes, well," the earl said briskly. "I won't stand for it. Gretham has been with me for three weeks shy of five years. You cannot imagine the trials I had to go through to find a man of business worthy of the title. To think that he would refuse further contact with me over a *gaming* hell, when I've got another one already in London, which he's had absolutely no problem with all these years..."

"*Patrick* Gretham?" she stammered as she put it all tougher. Patrick had quit his post rather than facilitate a sale of Siren's Retreat? She spun toward Stanley, her chest fluttering with hope. "You haven't signed a contract?"

Stanley held up a sheaf of papers. "We've *just* signed the contract."

Oh. Hot tears stung the backs of Deborah's eyes and her stomach hollowed with despair. Of course. What else should the earl be doing here, if not to sign a contract? Patrick's refusal hadn't stopped the river from flowing. It merely caused a new ripple to form.

Stanley raised his voice. "As I was saying, please help yourself to the brandy." He waited until the earl turned his back, and then lowered his voice, his eyes dancing with delight. "My daughters need never work another day in their lives. They shall possess formidable dowries now, and be the envy of debutantes everywhere."

Was she supposed to *congratulate* him on selling her home without the common courtesy to inform her of it first?

Yes, she realized with a sick feeling. Yes, that was exactly what he expected her to do. Selling Siren's Retreat at triple its value was an unthinkable windfall...for him. She couldn't even rail at him, accuse him of being selfish and greedy. The money was for his children, whom she adored—and who made singularly terrible assistants. They would do much better as wives. They would be *happier*.

Deborah ought to be happy for them, too. She was their aunt. Their favorite aunt. She loved them more than life itself.

And it was all she could do to keep from crying.

"Congratulations," she mumbled. The word stuck in her throat, refusing to come all the way out. It was swollen there, choking off her air supply, suffocating her. She opened her mouth and tried again, but this time no sound escaped at all.

The earl turned back from the buffet with two glasses of brandy in his hands. He held out the extra, not to Stanley, but to Deborah.

Good God, she could not be expected to *toast* him for his good fortune in acquiring and demolishing Siren's Retreat! She had hung the wallpaper herself, sewn every curtain, personally greeted every guest. All of the best moments of her life had taken place on that property. Her first love. Her second love. A thousand Cupid's arrows.

And now he would take a mallet to those cherished walls, and dismantle the best thing she had ever been part of.

"*Please.*" The word ripped from her throat. She turned her back on Stanley to petition the earl directly. "You cannot destroy Siren's Retreat. It's more than an inn, more than a home. It's a haven that has blessed the lives of countless couples who had lost all hope, until their lonely hearts first caught sight of—"

"Spare me." The earl rolled his eyes. He drained one of the brandy glasses, then set it aside, turning his attention to the other.

Spare him? Spare *him*?

Her fingers clenched into fists, and she took a menacing step forward. "If you had any idea—"

"Oh, I have more than an idea," he drawled. "I have a twenty-eight-page letter, longer than any book I've ever read, as well as a stack of personal recommendations and testimonials from fellow lords, casual acquaintances, total strangers... Have you *seen* this thing?"

He hefted what appeared to be a bulging scrapbook off the sideboard.

"I... What?" she managed.

Lord Edgewick handed her the heavy book. "I got bored a quarter of the way through. Every letter says the same bloody thing."

She opened it at random. There was a note from her recent guests, the Viscount and Viscountess Summerton, who had fallen in love in Deborah's

Rose Cottage years before, only to fall deeper in love all over again just this past March.

Then a few words from a charming young surgeon and his new wife, saying they never would have met if it weren't for Siren's Retreat. On the next page, a declaration from a baroness in her own right, who had despaired of finding true love until she'd crossed the threshold into Deborah's inn. On the next page…

"What *is* this?" she said in wonder.

"Your guest registry, from the looks of it," Stanley said dryly. "Heavily annotated."

"I've two different cousins who appear to owe their matrimony to that inn of yours," the earl said with obvious disdain. "I didn't even know they'd *been* to Brighton. Their overwrought prose is in there somewhere, if you keep flipping. Absolutely mortifying gooeyness."

She began to turn the page, then realized what he'd just said. "This inn of…*mine*, my lord?"

"Well, I can't turn it into a proper gambling den now, can I? Not when the deuced land it sits on bears a reputation as a magical place for lovers to unite. Not at all the atmosphere I was hoping to inspire. Wouldn't have seen it that way, if it weren't for my man of business's letter. That's in there, too, if you want to bore yourself witless. The man can't make a simple statement without adding three charts and eight affidavits to prove each claim."

She stared at the earl, unable to believe her ears.

Hope, terrible and wonderful, clawed back into her chest. "Siren's Retreat will remain standing?"

"It will if I have anything to say about it," Edgewick said gruffly. "That was Gretham's advice, too. Better to be admired as the patron of a beloved landmark, he says, rather than reviled for destroying the pet memories of the very pockets I was hoping to bilk."

She blinked. "Patrick said...that?"

Might he actually be...oh, of course not. But... what if he was?

The earl flapped his fingers dismissively. "Gretham blathered something along those lines. I'm paraphrasing. The man gets so *wordy* when he's worked up about some cause he's passionate for. I skimmed the important bits, as always. You don't know where Gretham has gone off to, do you?"

"I... No, I'm afraid I've no idea where he is." She hugged the heavy book to her chest and wished with all her might that it was Patrick.

"He included a ranked list of the second-best locations to open a gaming hell. I suppose I shall make do with that. But I refuse to settle for the second-best man of business without a fight." The earl gestured toward Deborah with his newly emptied wine glass. "Well, if you're not going to have a drink, at least take a pen and sign."

"Sign?" Her blood rushed in giddiness. "What are the new terms of the lease?"

The earl looked down his nose at her. "Lease? What lease? I'm not a patron of destiny or whatever hogwash Gretham was gibbering about if *you're* paying *me*. The land will be placed in a trust in your name, listing myself as beneficiary in the event of your death—"

She let out a garbled choke somewhere between surprise and laughter.

"—lasting for the duration of your natural life, on condition you do *not* tear down a single wall, with the exception of renovation and expansion. Siren's Retreat must remain standing and operational at all times, or the property reverts to me. If you're amenable to these terms—"

Deborah floated over to Stanley's desk, heavy tome be damned. "Where do I sign?"

CHAPTER 20

here wasn't time to run home before her meeting with LostInLondon, so Deborah found herself dashing up the walkway to the Old Ship Inn with no yellow flower, and a scrapbook clenched to her chest.

The earl hadn't wanted to take the book back with him, and Stanley had no use for it. Deborah had been horrified to learn their plan was to toss it into the fire like refuse. From now on, it would live on top of her reception counter right next to the guest registry. Any tourist wavering on making a reservation would be invited to peruse those pages whilst they thought it over. She'd be booked for the next ten years in no time.

And all of the existing reservations! Deborah would not have to write awkward, heartrending letters, pleading for forgiveness for cancelling holiday after holiday. Or raise the rates to astro-

nomical sums. Every hopeful heart could visit
Siren's Retreat as planned.

Deborah sprinted down the corridor and into
the coffee room. She startled to see Patrick seated at
one of the tables. All of the other chairs were empty.
She rushed over to him at once.

"Lord Edgewick is looking for you!" she blurted
out.

It was not how she meant to begin, nor what
she'd meant to say at all. Her mind was still jumbled
with the events of the past hour.

Patrick jerked his gaze toward hers and sprang
to his feet at once. "What?"

"The Earl of Edgewick. Never mind about him.
I've just discovered…" Her voice choked up, and she
held the scrapbook aloft. "Oh, Patrick, *you* did this!"

He shook his head in denial, his hazel eyes
bright with emotion.

"No, my love," he said softly. "*You* did that. Every
grateful, joyous word in that book is because of you."

Her cheeks flushed. She opened the album to
hide it. "Not every word. There's a letter in here
somewhere from a certain man of business who…"

There it was. The twenty-eight-page letter from
the missing man of business.

Written in a gorgeous script she'd recognize
anywhere.

She glanced up sharply, noting belatedly
Patrick's fine attire, his carefully groomed hair, the
bright yellow flower affixed to his lapel.

Daffodils. Her favorite.

"It *was* you." Her cheeks were suddenly wet. "It *is* you."

He touched her cheek. "Don't cry, Salt&Sea."

"Oh, LostInLondon," she whispered. "How I was hoping it would be you."

She set the book aside in order to twine her arms about his neck and hold on tight. He wrapped his arms about her tight.

"I've nothing to offer you but myself," he murmured into her hair. "And my life, and my love, and my very breath. I've left a lucrative post to find myself unemployed and homeless, making me a poor bargain indeed. But if you could find it within yourself to give me another chance, I will spend every heartbeat I have left in pursuit of your happiness, now and forevermore."

"You might not have quit as cleanly as you think," she warned him. "There's an earl out there willing to pay any price necessary for the safe return of his number one man of business."

"Is that what you want?" Patrick pulled back just far enough for his eyes to meet hers. "Whatever it is you desire, you need only to say the word."

"Whatever I need?" Was she choking? Laughing? Crying? She cupped his handsome face and smiled up at him blurrily. Wonderful, impossible man. "Now that you mention it, the proprietress of a certain inn appears to be in the market for a new assistant…"

He kissed her cheeks. "Your servant, from this day forth."

"Not a servant," she corrected him. "A partner. In all things."

He waggled his eyebrows. "...*All* things?"

"*All* things." She allowed her grin to widen wickedly.

He tucked her fingers around one elbow and lifted the scrapbook with his other arm. "I don't suppose you know of a bed with vacancy for the night?"

"Half a bed," she answered primly. "Are you willing to share?"

"For the rest of my life, if you'll have me."

"I'll think about it," she teased. "Ask me in the morning."

Deborah and Patrick ran to Siren's Retreat arm-in-arm. They did not emerge from her bedchamber until well after noon.

The legend had come true yet again.

WANT MORE romantic men and strong-willed women?

Try Nobody's Princess, the newest Regency heist caper in the Wild Wynchesters series. Keep turning for an excerpt!

DON'T FORGET your free book:

Click here for a bonus historical romance!

DID you miss the first book in the series?

What happens when a wife determined to leave her husband must share a honeymoon cottage with him, and his heart's desire is to rekindle the romance? Find out in A Tryst by the Sea!

THANK YOU

AND SNEAK PEEKS

MORE FREE BOOKS

Start a new series for FREE!

THE WILD WYNCHESTERS

This fun-loving, caper-committing family of tight-knit siblings can't help but find love and adventure. Why seduce a duke the normal way, when you can accidentally kidnap one in an elaborately planned heist?

Grab the first book here:
The Governess Gambit

"Erica Ridley is a delight!"
—Julia Quinn

"Irresistible romance and a family of delightful scoundrels... I want to be a Wynchester!"
—Eloisa James

ROGUES TO RICHES

In the Rogues to Riches historical romance series, Cinderella stories aren't just for princesses...

First book FREE:
Lord of Chance

DUKES OF WAR

Roguish peers and dashing war heroes return from battle only to be thrust into the splendor and madness of Regency England.

First book FREE:
The Viscount's Tempting Minx

12 DUKES OF CHRISTMAS

Heartwarming Regency romps nestled in a picturesque snow-covered village. After all, nothing heats up a winter night quite like finding oneself in the arms of a duke!

First book FREE:
Once Upon a Duke

GOTHIC LOVE STORIES

Prefer atmospheric romance with dark heroes, strong emotion, and an edge of danger?

First book FREE:

Too Wicked to Kiss

MAGIC & MAYHEM

Want to try a trio of lighthearted, feel good romantic comedies? You'll love these fun, paranormal rom-coms!

First book FREE:

Kissed by Magic

NOBODY'S PRINCESS

A fun and feminist Regency romp from a master of the genre hailed as "a delight" by _Bridgerton_ author Julia Quinn.

Nothing happens in London without Graham Wynchester knowing. His massive collection of intelligence is invaluable to his family's mission of aiding those most in need. So when he deciphers a series of coded messages in the scandal sheets, Graham's convinced he must come to a royal's rescue. But his quarry turns out not to be a princess at all... The captivating Kunigunde de Heusch is anything but a damsel in distress, and the last thing she wants is Graham's help.

All her life, Kuni trained alongside the fiercest Royal Guardsmen in her family, secretly planning to become her country's first Royal Guards_woman_. This mission in London is a chance to prove herself worthy *without* help from a man, not even one as devilishly handsome as Graham. To her surprise, Graham believes in her dream as much as she does, which makes it harder to resist kissing him...and falling in love. But how can she risk her heart if her future lies an ocean away?

Get Yours: Nobody's Princess
(Keep turning for a sneak peek!)

SNEAK PEEK

NOBODY'S PRINCESS

Graham Wynchester lay next to a row of brightly covered tulips, his body parallel to the ground as he pushed up with his arms and slowly lowered himself back down. Upon sight of Kuni, he started to rise to his feet.

Kuni motioned for him to continue. She was more than familiar with press-up exercises. She sprinted lightly over to him and dropped into position at his side, lowering herself down and pressing back up, keeping time to his rhythm.

His eyes widened in obvious surprise.

"What? You thought the English were the only ones who know how to exercise their muscles in this way?" she asked archly.

"Knowing how to do a thing and actually doing the thing are not at all the same thing," he answered. "Every person in my household has *seen* me do this. You're the first to do it *with* me."

She pressed up in silence, proud of her years of

training and the strength of her body. Even before she'd been anywhere near the battlefield practice sessions, her brothers would tease her at the drop of a feather to stop whatever she was doing and show them five of these maneuvers with perfect posture. Or ten. Or twenty. She could do over a hundred now without a respite.

Before she was even halfway there, however, Graham sprang to his feet and held out his palm to her.

Ah! She knew what came next in Balcovia. After strength-building was hand-to-hand combat.

She placed her hand in his, gripping tight, then yanked her elbow backwards. Graham's body jerked towards her in surprise, which was all Kuni needed. She used his forward momentum to tumble him past her and onto the ground on his back. Even as the breath whooshed out of him, she was already dropping atop, her palms flat against his, pinning him beneath her and covering his body with hers.

"W-what?" he managed hoarsely.

"Was hand-to-hand combat not the next step in your routine?" she asked innocently. "That's how we do it in Balcovia."

His eyes shone. "I adore Balcovia."

Graham's lips were close enough to kiss, not that she would do any such thing. It was enough that her body pressed its full weight scandalously against him.

She should probably roll off and set him free.

Soon.

Any moment now.

Or not. Her limbs were frozen in place. All right, all right, her limbs were anything but frozen. *Molten.* Her limbs were molten. Her body had melted against him, molded itself to him, melded them into one.

She wasn't even conscious of the weight of her limbs anymore. He was the life raft supporting her amidst an ocean of green grass and frothy flowers. Despite the danger inherent in pressing one's curves against a man's hard body, she felt oddly safe with him.

Perhaps it was more that she *wanted* to taste a little of this danger. Swordplay and combat practice with the other soldiers had never felt life-or-death, but this...*this* felt viscerally real. Graham had invited her onto the battlefield, where she had promptly engaged him in battle. What happened next could determine whether they—

He flipped her so swiftly and so easily she did not even register his movement until she found herself pinned beneath him, her spine against the soft grass, her breath vanishing from her lungs in a whoosh powerful enough to rustle the curly black tendrils tumbling over his forehead.

Now it was his body pressing into hers. Wide shoulders, slender hips, muscular thighs—and perhaps a hint of mutual interest pulsing between them.

A proper miss would be shocked right into a swoon.

It was a good thing Kuni wasn't the least bit proper. She had not only *started* this, she intended to savor every second of it.

∼

Grab Yours:
Nobody's Princess

THANK YOU FOR READING

Love talking books with fellow readers?

Join the *Historical Romance Book Club* for prizes, books, and live chats with your favorite romance authors:

Facebook.com/groups/HistRomBookClub

And check out the official website for sneak peeks and more:

www.EricaRidley.com/books

ABOUT THE AUTHOR

Erica Ridley is a *New York Times* and *USA Today* best-selling author of witty, feel-good historical romance novels, including THE DUKE HEIST, featuring the Wild Wynchesters. Why seduce a duke the normal way, when you can accidentally kidnap one in an elaborately planned heist?

In the *12 Dukes of Christmas* series, enjoy witty, heartwarming Regency romps nestled in a picturesque snow-covered village. After all, nothing heats up a winter night quite like finding oneself in the arms of a duke!

Two popular series, the *Dukes of War* and *Rogues to Riches*, feature roguish peers and dashing war heroes who find love amongst the splendor and madness of Regency England.

When not reading or writing romances, Erica can be found riding camels in Africa, zip-lining through rainforests in Central America, or getting hopelessly lost in the middle of Budapest.

Let's be friends! Find Erica on:
www.EricaRidley.com

CPSIA information can be obtained
at www.ICGtesting.com
Printed in the USA
LVHW110849050522
717990LV00029B/362

9 781088 016404